A Spoonful of Poison

Also by M. C. Beaton

The Skeleton in the Closet

A Spoonful of Poison

An Agatha Raisin Mystery

M. C. BEATON

 St. Martin's Minotaur ✽ New York

Plea

This is a work of fiction. All of the characters, organizations, and events portrayed in this novel are either products of the author's imagination or are used fictitiously.

Title page photo © Alex Bramwell / Dreamstime.com

www.minotaurbooks.com

Library of Congress Cataloging-in-Publication Data

Beaton, M. C.
    A spoonful of poison : an Agatha Raisin mystery / M.C. Beaton.—1st
St. Martin's Minotaur ed.
      p. cm.
    ISBN-13: 978-0-312-34912-7
    ISBN-10: 0-312-34912-2
    1. Raisin, Agatha (Fictitious character)—Fiction. 2. Women private
investigators—Fiction. 3. Fasts and feasts—Fiction. 4. Poisoning—
Fiction. 5. Cotswold Hills (England)—Fiction. I. Title.
PR6053.H4535S76 2008
823'.914—dc22

                     2008023581

First Edition: October 2008

10 9 8 7 6 5 4 3 2 1

This book is dedicated to my three bookselling
angels at the Cotswold Bookstore,
Moreton-in-Marsh, Gloucestershire—Tony Keats,
David Whitehead and Nina Smith.

A Spoonful of Poison

Chapter One

M<small>RS. BLOXBY, WIFE OF THE VICAR</small> of Carsely, looked nervously at her visitor. "Yes, Mrs. Raisin is a friend of mine, a very dear friend, but she is now very busy running her detective agency and does not have spare time for—"

"But this is such a good cause," interrupted Arthur Chance, vicar of Saint Odo The Severe in the village of Comfrey Magna. "The services of an expert public relations officer to bring the crowds to our annual fête would be most welcome. Proceeds will go to restore the church roof and to various charities."

"Yes, but—"

"It would do no harm to just *ask*, now would it? It is your Christian duty."

"I hardly need to be reminded of my duty," said Mrs. Bloxby wearily, thinking of all the parish visits, the mothers' meetings and the Carsely Ladies' Society. Really, she thought, surveying the vicar, for such a mild, inoffensive-looking man he is terribly pushy. Arthur

Chance was a small man with thick glasses and grey hair which stuck out in tufts like horns on either side of his creased and wrinkled face. He had married a woman twenty years his junior, Mrs. Bloxby remembered. He probably bullied her into it, she thought.

"Look! I will do what I can, but I cannot promise anything. When is the fête?"

"It is a week on Saturday."

"Only about a week away. You are not giving Mrs. Raisin any time."

"God will help her," said Mr. Chance.

Agatha Raisin, a middle-aged woman who had sold up her successful public relations business to take early retirement in a cottage in the Cotswolds, had found that inactivity did not suit her and so had started up her own private detective agency. Now that it was successful, however, she wished she had more time to relax. Also, the cases which poured into the detective agency all concerned messy divorces, missing children, missing cats and dogs, and only the occasional case of industrial espionage. She had begun to close the agency at weekends, feeling she was losing quality time, forgetting that when she had plenty of quality time, she didn't know what to do with it.

For a woman in her early fifties, she still looked well. Her hair, although tinted, was glossy and her legs good.

Although she had small eyes, she had very few wrinkles. She had a generous bosom and a rather thick waist, which was her despair.

On Friday evening, when she arrived home, she fussed over her two cats, Hodge and Boswell, kicked off her shoes, mixed herself a generous gin and tonic, lit a cigarette, and lay back on the sofa with a sigh of relief.

She wondered idly where her ex-husband, James Lacey, was. He lived next door to her but worked as a travel writer and was often abroad. She rummaged around in her brain as usual, searching for that old obsession, that old longing for him, but it seemed to have gone forever. Agatha, without an obsession, was left with herself; and she forgot about all the pain and misery that obsession for her ex had brought and remembered only the brief bursts of elation.

The doorbell shrilled. Agatha swung her legs off the sofa and went to answer the door. Her face lit up when she saw Mrs. Bloxby standing there. "Come in," she cried. "I'm just having a G and T. Want one?"

"No, but I'd like a sherry."

Sometimes Agatha, often too aware of her slum upbringing, wondered what it would be like to be a lady inside and out like Mrs. Bloxby. The vicar's wife was wearing a rather baggy tweed skirt and a rose-pink blouse which had seen better days. Her grey hair was escaping from a bun at the back of her neck, but she had her usual air of kindness and dignity.

The pair of them, as was the fashion in the Carsely Ladies' Society, always called each other by their second names.

Agatha poured Mrs. Bloxby a sherry. "I haven't seen you for a while," said Agatha. "It's been so busy."

A brief flicker of guilt crossed Mrs. Bloxby's grey eyes. "Have you still got that young detective with you, Toni Gilmour?"

"Yes, thank goodness. Excellent worker. But I think we will need to start turning down cases. I really don't want to take on more staff."

Mrs. Bloxby took a sip of sherry and said distractedly, "I knew you would be too busy. That's what I told him."

"Told who?"

"Mr. Arthur Chance. The vicar of Saint Odo The Severe."

"The what?"

"An Anglo-Saxon saint. I forget what he did. There are so many of them."

"So how did my name come up in your discussion with Mr. Chance?"

"He lives in Comfrey Magna—"

"Never been there."

"Few people have. It's off the tourist route. Anyway, they are having their annual village fête a week tomorrow and Mr. Chance wanted me to beg you to publicize the event for them."

"Is there anything special about this vicar? Any reason why I should?"

"Only because it's for charity. And he is rather pushy."

Agatha smiled. "You look like a woman who has just been bullied. Tell you what, we'll drive over there tomorrow morning and I will tell him one resounding *no* and he won't bother you again."

"That is so good of you, Mrs. Raisin. I am not very strong when it comes to saying no to good works."

In the winter days, when the rain dripped down and thick wet fog covered the hills, Agatha sometimes wondered what she was doing buried under the thatch of her cottage in the Cotswolds.

But as she drove off with Mrs. Bloxby the following morning, the countryside was enjoying a really warm spring. Blackthorn starred the hedgerows, wisteria and clematis hung on garden walls, bluebells shook in the lightest of breezes, and a large blue sky arched overhead.

Mrs. Bloxby guided Agatha through a maze of country lanes. "Here we are at last," she said finally. "Just park in front of the church."

Agatha thought Comfrey Magna was an odd, secretive-looking village. There were no new houses to mar the straggling line of ancient cottages on either side of the road. She could see no one on the main street or in the gardens or even at the windows.

"Awfully quiet," she commented.

"Few young people, that's the problem," said Mrs. Bloxby. "No first-time buyers, only last-time buyers."

"Shouldn't think houses would be all that expensive in a dead hole like this," said Agatha, parking the car.

"Houses all over are dreadfully expensive."

They got out of the car. "That's the vicarage over there," said Mrs. Bloxby. "We'll cut through the church-yard."

The vicarage was an old grey building with a sloping roof of old Cotswold tiles, the kind that cost a fortune but that the local council would never allow anyone to sell, unless they were going to be replaced with exactly the same thing, which, of course, defeated the purpose.

As they entered the churchyard, Agatha saw a man straightening up from one of the graves where he had been laying flowers. He turned and saw them and smiled.

Agatha blinked rapidly. He was tall, with fair hair, a lightly tanned handsome face, and green eyes. His eyes were really green, thought Agatha, not a fleck of brown in them. He was wearing a tweed sports jacket and cavalry-twill trousers.

"Good morning," said Mrs. Bloxby pleasantly, but giving Agatha's arm a nudge because that lady seemed to have become rooted to the spot.

"Good morning," he replied.

"Who was that?" whispered Agatha as they approached the door of the vicarage.

"I don't know."

Mrs. Bloxby rang the bell. The door was opened by a tall woman wearing a leotard and nothing else. Her hair was tinted aubergine and worn long and straight. She had rather mean features—a narrow, thin mouth and long narrow eyes. Her nose was thin with an odd bump in the middle, as if it had once been broken and then badly reset. Pushing forty, thought Agatha.

"You've interrupted my Pilates exercises," she said.

"We've come to see Mr. Chance," said Mrs. Bloxby.

"You must be the PR people. You'll find him in the study. I'm Trixie Chance."

Oh dear, thought Mrs. Bloxby. She often thought that trendy vicars' wives did as much to reduce a church congregation as a trendy vicar. Mrs. Chance was of a type familiar to her: always desperately trying to be "cool," following the latest fads and quoting the names of the latest pop groups.

Trixie had disappeared. By pushing open a couple of doors off the hall, they found the study. Arthur Chance was sitting behind a large Victorian desk piled high with papers.

He rushed round the desk to meet them, his pale eyes shining behind thick glasses. He seized Agatha's hands. "Dear lady, I knew you would come. How splendid of you to help us!"

Agatha disengaged her hands. "I have come here," she began, "to say—"

There was a trill of laughter from outside, and through the window Agatha could see Trixie talking to that handsome man.

"Who is that man?" she demanded, pointing at the window.

Arthur swung round in surprise. "Oh, that is one of my parishioners, Mr. George Selby. So tragic, his wife dying like that! He has been a source of strength helping me with the organization of the fête, ordering the marquees in case it rains. So important in our fickle English climate, don't you think, Mrs. Raisin?"

"Certainly," gushed Agatha. "Perhaps, if you could call Mr. Selby in, we could discuss the publicity together?"

"Certainly, certainly." Arthur bustled off. Mrs. Bloxby stifled a sigh. She knew her friend was now dead set on another romantic pursuit. She wished, not for the first time, that Agatha would grow up.

George Selby entered the study behind the vicar. He smiled at Agatha. "Are you sure you want to do this?" he asked. "Mr. Chance can be very persuasive."

"It's no trouble at all," said Agatha, thinking she should have worn a pair of heels instead of the dowdy flat sandals she was wearing.

But Agatha's heart sank as the events were described to her. There was to be entertainment by the village band and dancing by a local group of morris men. The rest consisted of competitions to see who had created the best cake, bread, pickles, and relishes. The main event was the home-made jam tasting.

She sat in silence after the vicar had finished outlining the events. She caught a sympathetic look from George's beautiful green eyes and a great idea leaped into her mind.

"Yes, I can do this," she said. "You haven't given me much time. Leave it to me." She turned to George. "Perhaps we could have dinner sometime in the coming week to discuss progress?"

He hesitated slightly. "Splendid idea," said the vicar. "Plan our campaign. There is a very good restaurant at Mircester. Trixie, my wife, is particularly fond of it. La Belle Cuisine. Why don't we all meet there for dinner on Wednesday? Eight o'clock."

"Fine," said Agatha gloomily.

"I suppose so," said George with a marked lack of enthusiasm.

Agatha's staff, consisting of detectives Phil Marshall, Patrick Mulligan, young Toni Gilmour and secretary Mrs. Freedman, found that the usual Monday-morning conference was cancelled. "Just get on with whatever you're on with," said Agatha. "I've got a church fête to sell."

Toni felt low. She had been given another divorce case and she hated divorce cases. But she lingered in the office, fascinated to hear Agatha Raisin in full bullying mode on the phone. "Yes, I think you should send a reporter. We're running a real food campaign here. Good home-village produce and no supermarket rubbish. And I can promise you a surprise. Yes, it *is* Agatha Raisin here. No, no murder, hah, hah. Just send a reporter."

Next call. "I want to speak to Betsy Wilson."

Toni stood frozen. Betsy Wilson was a famous pop singer. "Tell her it's Agatha Raisin. Hullo, Betsy, dear, remember me? I want you to open a village fête next Saturday. I know you have a busy schedule, but I also happen to know you are between gigs. The press will all be there. Good for your image. Lady-of-the-manor bit. Large hat, floaty dress, gracious—come on, girl, by the time I'm finished with you I'll have you engaged to Prince William. Yes, you come along and I'll see if I can get the prince." Agatha then charged on to tell Betsy to arrive at two o'clock and to give her directions to Comfrey Magna.

"Thick as two planks," muttered Agatha, "but she's coming."

"But she's famous!" gasped Toni. "Why should she come?"

"Her career was sinking after that drugs bust," said Agatha. "I did a freelance job and got her going again."

She picked up the phone again. "News desk? Forget about the healthy food. Better story. Fête is to be opened by Betsy Wilson. Yes. I thought that would make you sit up."

Toni waited until Agatha had finished the call and asked, "Can you really get Prince William?"

"Of course not, but that dumb cow thinks I'm capable of anything."

At dinner on the Wednesday night, only Trixie Chance greeted Agatha's news that Betsy Wilson was to open the fête with delight. George Selby said anxiously, "But the village will be overrun by teenagers and press. It'll be a disaster."

Agatha felt panicky. She now had the nationals coming as well as the local newspapers.

"I've got it," she said. "Vicar, you open the fête with a prayer. Get yourself a good sound system. Think of the size of the congregation. I'll get Betsy to sing 'Amazing Grace.' Set the tone."

The vicar's eyes shone. "I can see it now," he said, clasping his hands as though in prayer.

"Yes, so can I," said George. "Mess and rubbish everywhere."

Trixie squeezed his arm. "Oh, Georgy Porgy, don't be a great bear. Little Trixie is thrilled to bits."

She's five feet eight inches, thought Agatha sourly, and people who refer to themselves in the third person are always crashing bores.

"It'll be marvellous," said Agatha. "It'll really put Comfrey Magna on the map!"

She wondered how she could manage to engineer an evening with George on his own. Mustn't seem too *needy*. Men could smell needy across two continents.

In vain during the meal did George try to protest against the visit of the pop star. The vicar and his wife were too excited to listen to him.

What was worse, George was beginning to look at her with something like dislike in those grass-green eyes of his.

He leaned across the table, interrupting the vicar's enthusiastic plans and said coldly, "I've decided I don't really want to be part of this."

"But George," wailed Trixie, "we depend on you to organize the marquees and things."

"I am sure the very efficient Mrs. Raisin can take over from me. I only chipped in because Saint Odo's is a beautiful church and the fête was one way to raise funds towards the necessary repairs as well as sending some money to charity."

"Listen," said Agatha, panicking as gorgeous George seemed to be vanishing over the flat horizon of her present manless life, "here's an idea which will get you so much money you could build a cathedral. It will only mean one day of chaos. You put up barricades at the two roads leading into the village. You charge five pounds a head for entry. You get a couple of farmers, say, to contribute fields for parking. Haven't you any Boy Scouts or Girl Guides?"

"Yes, we do," said the vicar.

"Draft them in to park the cars and dib, dib whatever, you've got a fortune."

There was a startled silence. The vicar looked as if someone had just presented him with the Holy Grail. George gave a reluctant smile.

"I suppose it could work. We don't have much time."

"Call an emergency meeting in the village hall tomorrow," said Agatha eagerly.

"There are only a few days left," cautioned George.

"We can do it," said Agatha. "I know we can do it."

"What about all these crowds that are going to come? We'll need to inform the police."

Agatha quailed at the thought of her friend Detective Sergeant Bill Wong's reaction. "I'll do that," she said, "and I'll hire a security firm to police the area."

"You are an angel," said the happy vicar.

But George looked uneasy. "I feel no good will come of this," he said.

The dinner party finished at eight because the vicar liked to eat early and get to bed early.

Agatha cast one longing look after George's retreating well-tailored back as he headed for his car.

She must find out more about him. Surely Mrs. Bloxby knew something.

Later that evening, Mrs. Bloxby listened in alarm

to Agatha's plans. She felt that as Agatha had bulldozed ahead, there was now little point in making any protest. And when Agatha left, commenting on the incredible beauty of the Cotswolds spring, Mrs. Bloxby repressed a sigh. Agatha's perception of beauty, she felt, was prompted by her hormones. If only Agatha hadn't seen that handsome man in the graveyard. She knew her friend of old. Agatha was heading for another obsession, and while it lasted, the Cotswolds would be beautiful and every pop tune would have a special meaning.

Agatha sustained a visit from a very angry Bill Wong on Friday evening. "You might have told me first what your plans were," he complained, "and I would have done my best to stop you. Betsy Wilson! It's as bad as hiring Celine Dion for the occasion."

He was only slightly mollified by the news that Agatha had engaged a security firm that had promised to put as many of their men as possible on the ground.

Bill was the product of a Chinese father and a Gloucestershire mother. He had inherited his father's almond-shaped eyes, those eyes which were looking suspiciously at Agatha. "Who is he?" asked Bill.

"He? Who?"

"You've fallen for someone."

"Bill, can you not for once believe something good about me? I'm doing this for charity."

"So you say. I'll be there myself on Saturday."

"How's your love life?" countered Agatha. "Still dating my young detective, Toni Gilmour?"

"We go around together when we both get some free time, but . . ."

"But what?"

"Agatha, could you try to find out what she thinks of me? Toni is very affectionate and likes me, but there's no spark there, no hint of passion. Mother and father like her a lot."

Agatha eyed him shrewdly. "You know, Bill, you can't go after a girl just because your mother and father like her. Do you *yearn* for her?"

"Don't be embarrassing."

"All right. I'll find out what her intentions are."

"I'd better go. See you tomorrow."

Agatha, who had been sitting on a kitchen chair, rose with one fluid movement to show him out.

"You've had a hip replacement!" exclaimed Bill.

"Nonsense. It wasn't arthritis after all. A pulled muscle."

Agatha had no intention of telling Bill or anybody else that she had paid one thousand pounds at the Nuffield Hospital in Cheltenham for a hip injection. The surgeon had warned her that she would soon have to have a hip replacement, but now, free of pain, Agatha forgot his words. Arthritis was so ageing. She was sure it had been a pulled muscle.

George Selby had to admit to himself that it looked as if the day was going to be a success. Betsy Wilson was a rare pop singer in that she appealed to families as well as teenagers. He also had to admit that had she not arrived to open the fête, only a few people would have attended. What was considered the height of the fête was the tasting to find the best home-made jam. Little dishes of jam were laid out, and people tasted each and then dropped a note of their favourite in a ballot box.

The sun shone from a cloudless sky on the beauty of spring. It had been a cold, damp early spring, and now, with the sudden heat and good weather, it seemed as if everything had blossomed at once: cherry and lilac, wisteria and hawthorn and all the glory of the fruit trees in the orchards around the village.

Betsy Wilson, in a gauzy dress decorated with roses, made a short speech, clasped her hands and sang her latest hit, "Every Other Sunday." It was a haunting ballad. Her clear young voice floated up to the Cotswold hills. Even the hardened pressmen stood silently.

She sang two more ballads, finished by singing "Amazing Grace," and then was hustled into a stretch limo by her personal security guard. The band which had accompanied her packed up and left, to be replaced by the village band.

Then Toni, who was with Agatha, tugged her sleeve and said, "That's odd."

"What's odd?" asked Agatha.

"Look at all those teenagers queuing outside the jam tent."

"Really? If I thought it was going to be such a popular event, I'd have charged an extra admission fee."

"Could someone be peddling drugs inside that tent?" asked Toni.

"Why?"

"Some of the people coming out look stoned."

Agatha was about to walk towards the tent when she heard screams and commotion coming from over by the church. People were pointing upwards. A woman was standing at the top of the square Norman tower, her arms outstretched. As Agatha ran over to the church, followed by Toni, she heard someone say, "It's old Mrs. Andrews. Her said something about how her could fly."

Agatha saw George running into the church and ran after him, with Toni pounding after her. George was disappearing through a door at the back of the church where stairs led to the tower. Agatha ran up the stairs, panting and gasping as she neared the top. She staggered out onto the roof.

Mrs. Andrews was standing up on the parapet. "I can fly," she said dreamily. "Just like Superman."

George made a lunge for her—but too late.

With an odd little laugh, Mrs. Andrew sailed straight off into space. George, Agatha and Toni craned their heads over the parapet. Mrs. Andrew lay smashed on a table tombstone, a pool of dark blood spreading from her head.

George was white-faced. "What on earth came over her? She was a perfectly sane woman."

"The jam," said Toni suddenly. "I think someone's put something in the jam."

"Get down there," said Agatha, "and tell the security guards to seal off that damned tent."

She was about to run after Toni when George caught her arm. "What's this about the jam?"

"Toni noticed that an awful lot of teenagers were queuing up outside the jam tent and coming out looking stoned. I've got to get down there."

When they arrived outside the church, a woman came up to them looking distraught. "Get an ambulance. Old Mrs. Jessop's jumped into the river."

Police were beginning to shout through loudhailers that everyone was to stay exactly where they were until interviewed.

"Thousands of them," gasped Toni. "I told Bill there was something wrong with the jam."

Chapter Two

SIR CHARLES FRAITH, a friend of Agatha's, placed his slippered feet on a footstool in his drawing room and switched on the television to BBC news.

Agatha's frantic face seemed to leap at him out of the screen. "I don't know what happened," she was saying to the interviewer. "I think some maniac put something in the jam."

The interviewer went on to describe the events at Agatha's disastrous church fête. Apart from Mrs. Andrews and Mrs. Jessop, two villagers had suffered heart attacks.

The camera panned out over the village. It looked as if the whole of the county's police force were on the scene, busy taking down names and addresses. They'll never forgive Agatha for the expense of all this manpower, thought Charles. I'll get over there this evening and pick up the pieces.

As dusk settled down over the Cotswolds and blossoms glimmered whitely in the fading light, all was peace and quiet except at Comfrey Magna.

Inside the tent, lit by the harsh glare of halogen lights, the two organizers of the jam tasting, a Mrs. Glarely and a Mrs. Cranton, sat weeping quietly.

Agatha and Toni were being interviewed inside the tent for what seemed to Agatha like the hundredth time.

Facing her was Detective Inspector Wilkes, flanked by Detective Sergeant Collins. Bill Wong had been sidelined by Collins, a nasty, pushy woman, who had pointed out to Wilkes that Bill was tainted by his friendship with Agatha and should be kept out of the interview. Collins had said she was transferring to the Metropolitan Police, but Bill had a sinking feeling that she'd been turned down. Behind Agatha, waiting to be interviewed again, were the vicar, his wife and George.

"Now this Betsy Wilson," said Wilkes, "she was involved in some drug scandal a few years ago."

"She's clean," said Agatha, "and she didn't go near the jam tent. Betsy went straight to the platform. Her band had arrived earlier and set up. She sang her songs and left."

"What about the members of the band?" rasped Collins. Her hair was pulled back so severely that Agatha was amazed her eyes didn't water. "That lot are always into drugs. Assuming it was drugs and not some nasty local herb in the preserves."

"I think it was LSD," said Toni suddenly. "I've been thinking about it. It's a hallucinogen."

"And how come you know about it, young lady?" demanded Wilkes.

"It was a case we turned over to Worcester CID earlier this year," said Toni. "Do you remember, Agatha? A mother thought her son was on drugs. I followed him to that club in Evesham and found they were giving out tabs quite openly. So I informed the police and the club was raided."

"What are tabs?"

"LSD is usually found on little squares of blotting paper called tabs," said Toni. "It's also a clear liquid. All someone had to do was tip a few drops into each of the jam-testing dishes. I gather the show was set up early in the morning and then the organizers went home for breakfast. It might be an idea to trace the source of the drug. LSD isn't all that common in the clubs these days. It's all Ecstasy or crack cocaine or heroin."

Toni was a pretty young girl aged eighteen. She had naturally fair hair. Collins threw her a look of dislike. "You seem to know a lot about drugs."

"It's my job," said Toni. "I'm a detective. You see, that's how I found out our two organizers had left the tent empty. Before the tent was opened to the public, the various jam dishes were covered with white cloths fastened with drawing pins. The tent was only opened to the public after Betsy had finished singing."

"It wasn't us," wailed Mrs. Glarely.

"We'll need the names of all the women who contributed jam," said Wilkes. He sighed. "Are there many?"

"Only six," said Toni, pulling out a notebook. "I have their names and addresses here."

"Good girl," said Wilkes, and Agatha felt a little stab of jealousy. She felt tired and jaded, and there was Toni looking as fresh as a daisy. Had George noticed Toni? That was the trouble with middle-aged men. They were allowed to fancy young girls. Middle-aged women fancying young men were called cradle snatchers.

"And," went on Toni, "Mrs. Cranton said apart from these ladies, the only people who came into the tent before it was officially opened were Mr. George Selby, the vicar and his wife, and a pig farmer called Hal Bassett—"

"What was a pig farmer doing in the jam tent before it was opened?" interrupted Wilkes.

"He was trying to get an advance taste. He eats home-made jam by the spoonful. Then there was Miss Triast-Perkins from the manor. She claimed that she wanted to be sure of decorum at all the events. She said that Mrs. Raisin was out to ruin the village by running the fête like a three-ringed circus."

Agatha hated being left out. "Could we continue all this in the morning?" she pleaded.

"And I need to let the marquee people come and collect the tents tomorrow," said George.

"Just a few more questions," snapped Collins.

And so it went on until nearly midnight, when they were all told they could go but to report to a mobile police unit which would be in place in the village in the morning.

As they all walked outside the tent, Agatha asked George, "Do you know how much we made?"

"The vicar is going to count the money. There must be thousands. Of course, any relatives of Mrs. Andrews and Mrs. Jessop must be compensated, not to mention any people who suffered ill health."

Agatha had been about to suggest she should be compensated for hiring the security firm, but decided it might sound callous. She was desperately wondering how to set up a date with George when she heard the vicar calling her.

Reluctantly she turned back as George hurried away. "Mrs. Raisin," said Arthur Chance, "this is a terrible business. I would like to hire your agency to find out who did this terrible thing."

Trixie protested. "There are police all over the place."

"Mrs. Raisin's agency has a good reputation," said the vicar firmly.

"I'll do it," said Agatha. "I feel responsible."

"So you should," said Trixie, tossing her long hair. "Where's George?"

"I think he's gone home," said Agatha. "I'll be back first thing in the morning."

She headed to where she had parked her car to find Toni waiting for her. "We've been employed," said Agatha. "I think you and I should concentrate on this case and leave Phil and Patrick to cope with the rest." Agatha suddenly remembered Bill's request. "How are you and Bill getting along?" she asked.

"Fine."

"Madly in love?"

"We're just friends. No fire lit. Not for me, not for him, but poor Bill thinks there should be something just because his mum and dad want it." Toni had wanted to leave the agency and join the police force, but she owed Agatha a great deal. Agatha had rescued her from a brutal home. Perhaps when this case was over, she might find the courage to leave.

"See you at the office," said Agatha, stifling a yawn. "Make it eight o'clock. I'll phone Phil and Patrick and get them there early as well."

As Agatha drove up to her cottage, she saw Charles's car parked outside. She frowned in irritation. She didn't feel like coping with Charles and she resented the way he used her cottage like a hotel.

She let herself in. Charles was asleep on the sofa, with the television still on. Agatha switched it off and went upstairs to bed without waking Charles. Sleep did not come easily. She tossed and turned, remembering the events of the catastrophic day. It had all started so well, good-natured crowds flooding into the village and over to a field where a stage had been set up for Betsy. How pretty she had looked with her filmy dress floating in the slightest of breezes. After Betsy had driven off, a great number of people had started to head away. Then the disaster of poor Mrs. Andrews's flight from the tower. Who had put LSD, if that's what it was, in the jam? She remembered Toni's concise report. Her young detective had really shown her up. But she, Agatha, had been running here and there, trying to get the security guards to contain the scene. She fell down at last into a nightmare where Trixie and George were laughing at her because she had turned up at the fête without a stitch on.

In the morning she stumbled out of bed, feeling immeasurably tired. She showered and dressed and hurried downstairs. Charles was still asleep on the sofa, the cats beside him. She scribbled a note, telling him to feed the cats and let them out into the garden and then she drove off to Mircester where she had her office.

Phil Marshall and Patrick Mulligan, who had been called in by Agatha that Sunday for an emergency meeting, groaned when Agatha said that she and Toni were going to handle the Comfrey Magna case. Phil Marshall was in his seventies and Patrick was a retired police detective.

"You'll need to hire someone else," said Patrick. "Phil

and I can't cope on our own with the workload. I know a retired detective."

"This is getting like the geriatric employment agency," snapped Agatha, and then seeing the look of hurt on Phil's face, said quickly, "Sorry about that. Yes. Hire him. Mrs. Freedman will set up a contract for him." Mrs. Freedman, the secretary, gave a little smile. They had already discussed the idea of hiring someone extra before Agatha arrived, and the retired detective was one of her cousins. Agatha went through the files and allocated work for Monday morning and then turned to Toni. "We'd better be off to the scene of the crime. It'll be crawling with press, although a lot of them will be doorstepping Betsy in London." She bit her lip in vexation. She hadn't had time to look at the Sunday morning's papers, but she was sure they would have raked up all that old drug scandal about Betsy. Must get the vicar to say something about Betsy being a saint, she thought.

When Toni and Agatha arrived back at Comfrey Magna, they avoided the mobile police unit and went straight to the vicarage, battling their way through the press.

To Agatha's delight, George answered the door.

"Mr. Chance is in the study with my accountant. We're counting up the money."

Agatha followed George into the study, looking

dreamily at his back. He was wearing a shirt as blue as the sky above, chinos and shoes which looked as if they had been handmade.

"Ah, Mrs. Raisin!" cried the vicar, running around his desk to take Agatha's hands in his. "We have a fortune here. Various charities will get a generous sum, the church roof will be repaired, and then we will compensate the families of the bereaved."

"How much?" asked Agatha.

"Oh, let me introduce our accountant. Mrs. Raisin, or may I call you Agatha?"

"Please do."

"Agatha, I would like to introduce Mr. Arnold Birntweather. He lives in our village and has kindly offered his services. Tell her how much we have."

"We have thirty thousand pounds," said Arnold.

He was a very small man, with a dowager's hump and small eyes magnified by thick glasses. His hair was an improbable brown.

Again, Agatha was tempted to suggest that they pay her for the services of the security firm and then again decided it would look too mean. Also, any builder these days with the expertise to repair the church roof would take most if not all of the money.

"Where is Trixie?" asked Agatha, looking around for what she had privately damned as the "competition."

"My poor wife has gone to the hairdresser. She has been so shocked by the events of yesterday. She felt like some type of beauty treatment to calm her nerves. Now I must get to the church for morning service."

"Could you please say a few words to the press outside after the service about Betsy?" asked Agatha. "Something nice about such a famous pop star giving up her time?"

"Of course," said Arthur.

"I'll come with you," said George.

"Good idea," said Agatha brightly.

"Shouldn't we be out there interviewing people?" whispered Toni.

"They'll all be in church," muttered Agatha as the vicar rushed off, clutching his sermon.

The church of Saint Odo The Severe had not escaped the attentions of Cromwell's troops. There was no stained glass in the windows and bright shafts of sunlight shone through mullioned panes of clear glass. The church was full. Toni fretted. Instead of getting on with the job, they were now trapped inside for a full morning service.

Agatha wondered where the vicar's wife had managed to find a hairdresser on a Sunday.

As the service dragged on, Agatha's conscience began to get the better of her. George was in the pew in front and all she could do was stare at the back of his head.

She pinched Toni's arm in the middle of a rendering

of "Abide with Me" and jerked her head to indicate they should leave.

They both emerged, blinking in the sunlight. Boy Scouts and Girl Guides—or did they call them Girl Scouts these days?—were moving about the village, filling up plastic bags with rubbish. Either they had drafted in troops from surrounding villages, thought Agatha, or this was a very fecund village. "We'll start with Hal Bassett, the pig farmer," said Agatha.

She stopped one of the Scouts and asked the boy if he knew where Bassett's pig farm was. "I don't come from here," said the boy, moodily poking a plastic bag with a pointed stick. "Ask her over there, the girl with the carroty hair. She's from here."

The girl when questioned said that Hal Bassett's farm was outside the village up on the hill to the left.

"Is it far?" asked Agatha. She was wearing high-heeled sandals.

"No," said the girl, pointing to the left. "You go along to the end of the village and walk straight up the hill. You'll see a sign to the farm. It's called Bassett's Piggery. You can't miss it. It smells."

"What if he's in church?" asked Toni as they set off.

"Don't think so." Agatha had convinced herself that a jam-loving pig farmer would not be religious.

It was a long straggling village, possibly built along one of the old drove roads. The church was at one end and the road leading to the farm at the other. The small cottages on both sides of the road did not have any gardens at the front. They seemed to crouch beside the road, small, old and secretive. Nobody moved on the deserted main street. Unlike Carsely, there were no streets leading off the main one. One main street was all there was to Comfrey Magna. In a few gaps between the houses, Agatha could see gardens at the back full of spring blossom, but no one had thought to plant anything in the little bit of earth between the houses and the road in the front. The place was deserted.

The street was cobbled. A heel of Agatha's sandal got stuck between the cobbles and was wrenched off.

"You wait here," said Toni. "I'll run back and get the car."

Agatha enviously watched her flying figure as Toni raced off down the street. Toni's fair hair gleamed in the sunlight. She was wearing jeans and a T-shirt and flat sandals. Why did I get all dressed up? mourned Agatha in all the glory of a mustard-coloured linen suit with a short skirt. Because you wanted to get Gorgeous George's attention, said the inner governess. Agatha was not plagued by any inner child but by this governess, who yakked on, "Why were you so stupid? What do you know of George? Has he shown any wit, humour, charm or anything? No. So here you are, all dressed up like a dog's dinner."

Agatha began to wish Toni would hurry up. It was as if there was a feeling of dislike emanating from the very stones of the old cottages. She kept feeling there was a face at one of the windows, just seen out of the corner of her eye, but when she whipped round, the window was empty and blank.

She heaved a sigh of relief when she saw Toni arriving with her car at last. Agatha climbed in. "I've got a pair of flat shoes in the back," she said. "I'll put them on when we get to the farm."

The farm turned out to be nearly at the top of a very steep hill leading out of the village. "I bet he looks like one of his pigs," said Agatha. "All that jam. He's probably round and pink like a porker."

"It does pong something awful," said Toni when she drove into the farmyard.

"I hope he's at home after all this." Agatha put on a pair of flat sandals and flexed her toes with relief.

"It was a funny time of year for a jam tasting," said Toni. "I mean, you would think maybe after the strawberries came out."

"In this backward dump, they probably make jam out of weeds," said Agatha. "The farm door's open. Hullo! Anybody at home?"

A thin, commanding-looking woman dressed in jeans and a washed-up cotton blouse appeared in the doorway. She had thick grey hair, grey eyes and a thin mouth.

She looked Agatha up and down and sighed. "You Jehovahs," she said in an upper-class accent. "Dragging your poor children from door to door."

"I am not a Jehovah," snapped Agatha. "My name is Agatha Raisin and this is one of my detectives, Miss Toni Gilmour."

"Oh, so you're the female responsible for the deaths yesterday."

"Look," said Agatha, "I would like to speak to Mr. Bassett."

"I am Mrs. Bassett." Her eyes raked Agatha from head to foot. You could leave the Birmingham slum, thought Agatha, but it was always there, deep inside, waiting to make you feel inferior.

"It's Mr. Bassett I want to speak to." Agatha's small eyes bored truculently into Mrs. Bassett's face.

"Come in," she said abruptly.

They followed her into a kitchen which was like something out of the pages of *Cotswold Life* magazine. It shone and gleamed in the sunlight, from the latest utensils to the copper pots hanging on hooks above a granite counter.

"Wait there," commanded Mrs. Bassett, pointing towards a kitchen table surrounded by Windsor chairs.

She strode out the back door and called in stentorian tones, "Hal!"

There was a faint answering cry.

"He's coming," said Mrs. Bassett, striding back into the kitchen.

As usual, Agatha's eyes ranged around the room looking for an ashtray, but she could not see a single one.

Mrs. Bassett began to grind coffee beans. She had her back to them and seemed unaware of their very existence.

Hal Bassett came into the kitchen. Mrs. Bassett swung round. "Boots!" she said.

Hal retreated to the doorway, sat down on a small stool at the entrance and tugged off his green wellies.

"Who are they?" he asked.

"It's that Agatha Raisin woman and her sidekick," said Mrs. Bassett.

Hal walked up to the kitchen table, twisted a chair round and straddled it. I hate men who do that, thought Agatha.

He was a tall brown-haired man dressed in a checked shirt and cords. He smelt strongly of pig. "So you're the female responsible for the mayhem yesterday," he remarked. His voice was light and pleasant. He had a square regular face. He did not look at all like the kind of person to haunt a jam-tasting exhibition.

"I'm not responsible for the LSD in the jam—if that is what the drug was," said Agatha.

"What did you expect, encouraging a load of riff-raff to come here?" said Hal.

"It seems as if it had nothing to do with the visitors," said Agatha. "The exhibition was set up in the marquee early in the morning by the organizers, Mrs. Glarely and Mrs. Cranton. The only people to visit the tent before the opening were yourself, Miss Triast-Perkins, the vicar and his wife and Mr. Selby. Did you taste any of the jam?"

"No," said Hal. "I tried to buy a pot of plum jam from the ones on sale, but I was told I'd have to wait. Mrs. Cranton wouldn't let me try any of the samples until the place was open to the public. Fair carried away with all this pop-singer nonsense."

"Did you go back?"

"Couldn't. Got a sow in farrow. I had to get back here."

Toni smiled at him. "We aren't suggesting you had anything to do with it. Of course not. But we wondered whether you might have seen anything when you were in the marquee."

Hal smiled back. "What's a pretty thing like you doing being a detective? No, I didn't see anything out of the way. But if I remember something, I'll phone you. Got a card?"

Toni took out one of her business cards, but before he could take it, it was snatched by Mrs. Bassett, who said icily, "Hal has work to do. If you've finished, we'd like to get on."

They were just getting into the car in the farmyard when Hal came hurrying out. He thrust a packet of sausages at Toni. "Here you are," he said. "Prime pork. My own pigs."

"That's very kind of you," said Toni. "Does it always pong like this round here?"

He laughed. "I've got a load of pig muck stacked up to sell to the farmers for fertilizer. It'll be cleared out tomorrow. My pigs don't smell. Come back sometime and I'll give you a tour."

"Hal!" called Mrs. Bassett from the doorway.

"Coming."

"You've made a conquest there," said Agatha, feeling low. How great it would be to be young and pretty like Toni. George would surely pay attention to her.

"George was in the tent as well," said Toni. "I forgot about that. Do you know anything about him?"

"No, only that his wife died."

"Maybe he poisoned her."

"Just drive," said Agatha sourly. "And find the manor house. We'd better have a word with Miss Triast-Perkins."

Toni drove back down into the village. "Aren't we supposed to be reporting to the police?"

"Later."

People were returning from the church service. Toni lowered the window and asked for directions to the manor, and was told it was at the other end of the village, just beyond the church. "Did you see the way they were all looking at us?" asked Toni. "They're all in their Sunday best, but if you put them in, say, medieval dress, their faces would fit. They looked as if they would really

like to lynch us. I bet there's a lot of nasty things go
on behind closed doors here—wife beating, incest and
drunkenness.

"Or maybe they're too God-fearing to get up to anything nasty," said Agatha. "Anyway, I could imagine one
of them poisoning the jam with some nasty poisonous
plant. But LSD? I don't think any of them would even
know where to get it."

"Oh, oh." Toni braked suddenly.

"What is it?"

"Bill's waving us over to the mobile police unit."

Another hour and a half of rigorous questioning by
Collins and Wilkes left Agatha beginning to feel as if
she had put the LSD in the jam herself.

When she and Toni were finally allowed to go, Agatha
looked around, hoping to see a sign of George, but he
was nowhere to be seen.

They got in the car and drove to the manor house.
The large iron gates were propped open. Beside the
gates was a lodge house, fallen into disrepair. "I wonder
why the lodge was left like that," said Agatha. "With
the clamour for housing these days, you'd think she'd
have sold it off."

The manor house was a square Georgian building, the
front of which was covered by the twisting branches of
an old wisteria just coming into flower. Like the village,

it had a blank, secretive air. Several of the windows had been blocked up from the days when owners tried to avoid the window tax.

They got out of the car and Agatha rang the bell. They waited patiently. Turning round, Toni noticed that the garden was unkempt—just a weedy lawn and several bushes planted around it.

The door opened. "Are you Miss Triast-Perkins?" asked Agatha.

She was a small thin woman with grey hair worn straight from a centre parting. Her face was thin and her large eyes were pale blue. She was wearing a faded print summer dress.

"You are that woman who organized the fête," she said. "You'd better come in."

They followed her into a gloomy sitting room where nothing seemed to have been changed since Victorian times: heavy furniture, stuffed birds in glass cases, framed photographs, and a grand piano covered by a fringed shawl.

"You were in the jam-tasting exhibition before it opened," began Agatha. "I wonder if you noticed anyone lifting the covers over the jam."

"No. I asked Mrs. Glarely if I could see that my marmalade was in a prominent position, but she went all bossy and refused to let me see. Those normally quiet sheepish women can turn quite bullying when they are put in charge of anything. Mr. Bassett came in to see if he could get a taste, but she refused him as well. Mr. Bassett and I talked to the vicar and that silly wife of his, who had just turned up. Oh, and dear Mr. George Selby. Poor man. He does mourn for his wife. She was such a pretty woman and did a lot of work for the parish."

"How did she die?" asked Agatha.

"The poor thing fell downstairs. She was carrying a tray of things and missed her footing. George is an architect and I'd warned him about those stairs. He has an old cottage near the church. Very old staircase, stone, you know, with deep steps."

"When did this happen?"

"Last year, in June. I don't think he'll ever marry again. No one could match up to Sarah."

"Sarah being his late wife?"

"Yes."

"And she was pretty?"

What on earth was Agatha doing? wondered Toni.

"Oh, so dainty. A little slip of a thing."

Agatha began to feel large and lumpy.

Toni said, "The problem is this. We believe that someone put LSD into the jam-tasting dishes. But the young people at the fête did not begin to queue up, having heard there was some drug available, until after the damage had been done. So it could very well have happened at the beginning, when the jam tasting was open to the public."

"You'll need to ask the organizers who was there. I went off to walk round the other displays."

"Where do Mrs. Cranton and Mrs. Glarely live?"

"On either side of the pub in the main street. Mrs. Glarely on the near side and Mrs. Cranton on the far side."

"If you can think of anything at all that might help, please phone me," said Agatha, handing over her card.

Outside, Toni asked, "Why all the questions about George?"

"He was in the tent at the beginning," said Agatha defensively.

"I've been thinking," said Toni, "it wouldn't take much effort to slide some LSD into the jam. It's a clear liquid. Instead of tabs of the stuff, someone could have had a small flask concealed in the palm of their hand. There are too many suspects. How are we ever going to find out who did it?"

"We'll just need to push on." Agatha took the wheel this time, but as they were approaching the vicarage, she saw George going in and slammed on the brakes.

"Toni, I think it would be a good idea if you could go ahead and interview these ladies on your own. I want to check something with the vicar."

And she's just seen George going in to the vicarage, thought Toni. She really is in pursuit of that man. Aloud, she said cheerfully, "Just park the car. I'll walk."

When Toni had left, Agatha got a bag of make-up out of the glove compartment and repaired her face and brushed her hair.

The vicarage door was open. She walked in, hearing the sound of voices coming from the back of the house. Through the kitchen window she saw, to her dismay, not only George and the vicar and his wife but Charles Fraith. They were sitting round a garden table under the shade of a cedar tree, chatting animatedly. Trixie Chance had turned into a blonde. Her long hair fell in golden waves to her shoulders. Where the hell did she get a dye job like that done on a Sunday? wondered Agatha. And blast and damn Charles.

As she approached the group, Charles called out, "Hi, Aggie. Why didn't you wake me up when you got home last night?"

Trixie looked amused. As Agatha sat down in a chair at the table, Trixie asked, "Are you pair an item?"

"Just friends," snapped Agatha.

"Thought so. Bit young for you."

Agatha was in her early fifties and Charles in his forties. She decided she actually hated Trixie. A breeze blew across the garden, sending a shower of petals from a fruit tree swirling across the grass. It blew a strand of

Trixie's golden hair onto George's shoulder. He was sitting very close to her.

"How have you been getting on with the investigation?" asked Charles.

"Not very far. The list of suspects gets longer and longer."

"I wonder if it was simply one kind of jam that had the LSD in it," said Charles. "If they could find that out at the autopsy, we could focus on the person who made that jam."

"Won't work," said Agatha. "Too many people were getting stoned. Toni says someone could have had a small flask of the stuff. Maybe the police should try to trace where that came from. Can't see the drug dealers selling flasks of the stuff."

"It also comes in gelatine squares," said Charles.

"How do you know that?"

"Googled it on your computer this morning," said Charles.

Charles looked as lazy and relaxed as always. He was wearing a short-sleeved checked shirt and jeans of that soft expensive blue look which costs a fortune. His fair hair was barbered and his neat features looked amused as he glanced from Agatha around the group.

"I came to help you," he said to Agatha. "Perhaps we should start with the jam makers."

"Toni's talking to two of them, so that leaves four."

Agatha took out her notebook. "No, it leaves two. Mrs. Andrews and Mrs. Jessop were jam makers. The two remaining ones are Miss Tubby and Miss Tolling. Was there a lot of competition amongst the jam makers?"

"I don't think so," said the vicar. "Mrs. Andrews usually won. Her chunky marmalade was superb."

"But there's another one," exclaimed Agatha. "Miss Triast-Perkins up at the manor. She said she had marmalade in the tasting."

"I forgot about her," said Trixie. "It's the first year she's entered anything."

"So where can we find Miss Tubby and Miss Tolling?" asked Charles.

"They live together," said the vicar.

"Lesbians," said Trixie, twisting a long strand of golden hair between beringed fingers.

"Now, dear," admonished Arthur. "I am sure it is all very innocent. They live in Rose Cottage, opposite the pub."

"I never saw a pub," said Agatha.

"It used to be a shop. It's set a little back from the road. Called the Grunty Man."

"Odd name."

"Probably was the Green Man at one time."

"Where have all the press gone?" asked Agatha.

"The police decided they were interfering with the investigation and banished them from the village and they have stopped any more entering."

Toni had failed to get anything out of either Mrs. Glarely or Mrs. Cranton. At both addresses she was told by their husbands to "get lost." She wandered back down the village street in the sunshine.

Men were dismantling the marquees which had held the exhibits. She stood watching as they took down the jam tent. As the canvas collapsed, something small and glittering in the sunlight rolled out from the folds and lay on the grass. Toni ran forward. It was a small glass phial.

"Stop!" she screamed at the workers. "Evidence. Stop! Get the police."

The door of the mobile police unit opened and Bill Wong came out. "Over here, Bill," yelled Toni.

Bill ran to join her and Toni pointed to the phial on the grass. Bill put on a pair of latex gloves, took out an evidence bag, carefully lifted up the phial and popped it in the bag.

"Why didn't we see that before?" he asked.

"It fell out of the canvas when they were taking the marquee down," said Toni.

"You'd best come back with me and make a statement. Don't let Collins fluster you. She'll probably suggest you put it there yourself!"

Chapter Three

"TRIXIE'S QUITE ATTRACTIVE," commented Charles as he and Agatha walked along the village street.

"If you like ageing hippies," said Agatha waspishly.

"She has beautiful hair, you must admit that. Like Rapunzel?"

"Who?" demanded Agatha. Fairy stories had not been part of her deprived childhood.

"Never mind. Who's this George character?"

"Just some villager who was helping out with the fête," said Agatha casually, aware of Charles's searching eyes on her face.

"Single?"

"Widower."

"Aha!"

"Aha what?"

"You're off again."

"I don't know what you mean. There's the pub. It

looks like a converted shop. No wonder I didn't notice it before."

"And here's Rose Cottage. Ring the bell."

"There isn't one."

"So knock the knocker."

Agatha seized the brass knocker in the shape of a lion's head with a ring in its mouth and rapped hard.

A lace curtain beside the left-hand window twitched. Agatha waited impatiently for what she envisaged as a couple of elderly spinsters.

The door opened and a young woman stood there, hands thrust into a pair of worn jeans. She had a round rosy face and glasses and short hair in a gamine cut.

"Yes?"

"I'm looking for Miss Tubby and Miss Tolling," said Agatha.

"I'm Maggie Tubby. What do you want?"

"My name is Agatha Raisin. This is Sir Charles Fraith. I am a private detective who has been asked by your vicar to investigate what happened at the fête. I would like to ask you a few questions."

"You'd better come in. We're in the garden."

She led the way through the small cottage to a long garden at the back where a woman was weeding. "Phyllis!" called Maggie. "Visitors."

Phyllis straightened up and stood wiping her hands. Agatha guessed she was in her thirties. She was tall with prematurely grey hair and a catlike face. What a lot of grey hair there is around this place, thought Agatha. Do they never think of getting their hair tinted?

Maggie explained the reason for the visit. Phyllis indicated a garden table and chairs. "Let's sit down," she said.

"I gather you both contributed jam to the tasting," said Agatha.

"Yes, plum jam. It's our speciality."

"Did you taste any of the exhibits?"

"Oh, yes," said Maggie. "What a trip!"

"Which one was it?"

"It was Miss Triast-Perkins's marmalade. Everything went funny. I began to see flashing lights."

"Didn't you think to warn anyone?"

"I just thought the jam was badly preserved—like some people we know." Maggie shot a sly look at Phyllis. They both looked at Agatha and giggled.

I wish you precious pair had jumped off the tower, thought Agatha.

Charles asked, "Have you any idea who might have done such a thing?"

"Of course," said Phyllis.

"Who?" demanded Agatha eagerly.

"Why, none other than Sybilla Triast-Perkins."

"What proof have you?" asked Charles.

"Only that she has murdered before, so it was probably easy for the unhinged creature to murder again."

"Murdered who?" Agatha almost shouted the question.

"Sarah Selby, poor little thing."

"George Selby's wife? The one who fell downstairs?"

"Pushed," said Maggie.

"Then why wasn't she arrested?"

"No actual proof, and she's a friend of the chief constable. She was visiting at the time. She said that Sarah had gone up the stairs to fetch the breakfast tray. George always gave her breakfast in bed. She tripped, said Sybilla, and tumbled down onto the stone flags of the hall and broke her neck. But here's the thing. According to the rigor mortis, Sarah had been lying there dead for an hour before Sybilla called the ambulance and police."

"What was her excuse for not calling them immediately?" asked Agatha.

"Sybilla said that she fainted with shock and when she came to, she felt dizzy and sick and it took about an hour for her to get the strength to phone," said Phyllis.

"Why would she want to kill Sarah Selby?" asked Agatha.

Phyllis and Maggie exchanged glances. Phyllis said, "She was crazy about George. Always visiting his house on some pretext or other, but before that fatal visit, she never called except when George was at home. He has an office in Mircester, though sometimes he works from home. He's an architect."

"Does everyone in the village suspect her?" asked Agatha.

"No, only us. They're all a bit backward in this backwater. You know, tug their forelocks to the lady of the manor. Some lady. Okay, the Triasts were upper crust, but old man Perkins made his money out of biodegradable cats' toilets."

"Place looked a bit run-down," said Agatha.

"She's mean, that's why," said Maggie.

"So why doesn't she sell off that lodge house, for example?"

"Blessed if I know," said Maggie. "Maybe she concocts poisons there." She and Phyllis laughed heartily.

"And what do you do for a living?" asked Agatha. "Manufacture LSD?" She had not forgiven them for that "badly preserved" remark.

"I paint," said Phyllis, "and Maggie throws pots. Don't you feel a bit guilty? If it hadn't been for your grandiose ideas about the fête, this wouldn't have happened."

"If you think it was Sybilla who did it," said Agatha, "then it really doesn't matter how many people attended the fête."

She and Charles took their leave. As they walked back, Agatha plunged into a rosy dream. She would solve the case of Sarah Selby's death. She would break the news gently to George, holding his hands and gazing into his eyes.

"Thank you," he would breathe. "Now I have closure.

I thought poor Sarah could never be replaced, but now . . ."

"Wake up, Aggie," said Charles. "You're wandering along with a silly smile on your face."

"I was thinking about the case." Agatha was angry at having her dream interrupted. As they came in sight of the vicarage, Agatha saw George saying goodbye to Trixie. She laughed at something he said and kissed him on the cheek.

Hair extensions, thought Agatha. That's it. I must get hair extensions.

Toni came running to meet them and told Agatha about finding the phial. "Who ever put the LSD in the jam must have thrust the phial into one of the seams of the canvas," she said.

Agatha heard herself being hailed and turned round with a smile to greet George. "I'm very worried about all this. Have you any clues?" he asked.

"Got quite a few," said Agatha. An idea struck her. "Look, I'm busy at the moment. Here's my card. Why don't you come to my cottage in Carsely this evening for drinks, say at seven, and I'll fill you in."

"Right," said George, tucking the card into his top pocket. "I'll see you then."

Now, thought Agatha, I've got to get rid of Charles.

Agatha decided to call it a day. She told Toni and Charles that with all the press haunting the outside of the village and police crawling all over the place, it would be better to come back the following day, when things might have cooled off a bit.

Scouts were dumping bags of all the refuse they had collected outside the mobile police unit, and a squad of tired-looking policemen were starting to go through the bags.

She saw two elderly women being led to the police unit. "That's Mrs. Glarely and Mrs. Cranton, I think," said Toni. "I'll phone Bill tonight and see if he'll tell me what they said."

Agatha was just steeling herself to say something to Charles when he said, "I've got to go out tonight. Maybe see you later or tomorrow."

"Do you want me to do anything more today?" asked Toni. "Or will I stay here and scout around on my own?"

"See if you can collar Bill and get anything out of him," said Agatha, now anxious to leave and begin beauty preparations for the evening ahead.

But duty nagged and she knew she had better call in to her office before she went home.

Motherly Mrs. Freedman was serving a man with coffee and biscuits when Agatha arrived. "This is ex-Detective Sergeant Jimmy Wilson," she said. "Jimmy, your boss, Mrs. Raisin."

Jimmy was a medium-sized, pugnacious-looking man. He had a round face with small eyes and a squashed nose above a pursed mouth. To Agatha's relief, he seemed to be in his early fifties.

"Did you take early retirement?" she asked.

"I had cancer," said Jimmy. "By the time I got over it, I felt like taking a long break, so I resigned. But I'm fit and ready for work now. I've got good contacts with the police."

"We're overloaded with work," said Agatha, "but Mrs. Freedman will give you some jobs to get started on. Did you sign a contract?"

"Yes, my cousin here gave me all the papers."

"Cousin?" queried Agatha, scowling at Mrs. Freedman.

She blushed. "Well, you needed someone and I knew Jimmy here was a good detective."

"We'll see how you go," said Agatha. "I may want you to check with your police friends to find out anything you can about this business at Comfrey Magna. But we'll deal with that when you've cleared up some of the backlog. I've got to rush. I've got an important interview to do with the case I'm on."

Agatha had just removed a face pack and was washing her face when her doorbell rang. She cast an agonized look at her watch. Six o'clock. It couldn't be George. She towelled her face dry and ran downstairs and opened the door. It was Mrs. Bloxby.

"Oh, come in," said Agatha. "I'm expecting someone this evening for drinks and I was just cleaning myself up. Coffee? Sherry?"

"Nothing for me," said Mrs. Bloxby, following Agatha through to the kitchen. "You were asking about George Selby?"

"Yes," said Agatha. "In fact, he's coming here this evening for drinks."

"Why?"

"Because he wants to know how I'm getting on with the case," said Agatha tetchily.

"Do you know how his first wife died?"

"Yes, she fell down the stairs. A Miss Triast-Perkins was there, but evidently too shocked to phone for an ambulance until after an hour had passed."

"It's all gossip, of course," said Mrs. Bloxby reluctantly, "and you know how unreliable gossip can be."

"I heard about Miss Triast-Perkins having a crush on George."

"There's a bit more to it than that. The rumour is that Mr. Selby encouraged her attentions."

"How Victorian you sound! Encouraged her attentions, indeed."

"If you don't want to hear it . . ."

"Sorry. Yes, I do. Why should he encourage her? She's hardly a glamour puss."

"Miss Triast-Perkins is very rich. She does not like spending money, but it seemed that Mr. Selby had

encouraged her to let him draw up plans to rebuild the
lodge and make expensive alterations and repairs to the
manor. She then used this as a sort of bait to keep him
calling, dithering and delaying. Miss Triast-Perkins did
not call when Mr. Selby wasn't at home, and it is certainly odd that she called that day and so early in the
morning, as it was just after Mr. Selby had left. Also, at
that time Mr. Selby was in financial difficulties. He had
just completed an expensive job for someone who then
went bankrupt and couldn't pay. His wife's life was heavily insured. Village gossip, which can be very spiteful, as
you know, was that George, having become impatient at
getting the contract out of Miss Triast-Perkins, had more
or less promised to marry her if he were free, therefore
encouraging her to push his wife down the stairs. Oh, is
that the time? I really must get on."

And having delivered herself of that bombshell, Mrs.
Bloxby hurried off.

"Snakes and bastards," muttered Agatha, fleeing upstairs again. "Can't be anything in it."

But her anticipation and excitement over the evening
ahead had dwindled somewhat. She knew she had the
reputation of being a very rich woman. She would see.
If George started suggesting that he could remodel her
cottage, she would be prepared.

By seven o'clock, Agatha was ready for her visitor
dressed in a very short skirt, sheer stockings, white silk
blouse and very high heels.

When she opened the door to George, she found to her dismay that he was casually dressed in an open-necked striped shirt, well-worn sports jacket and chinos. She invited him into her sitting room, fixed him the whisky he requested, poured a gin and tonic for herself, and then wondered where to sit. She should never have worn stockings with a short skirt. If she sat on the sofa or armchair, her skirt would ride up, exposing stocking tops. Agatha settled for a seat on a hard upright chair.

George sat on the sofa and cradled his drink in his hands. "This is a bad business," he said moodily. "Any suspects?"

"At the moment, there's just one," said Agatha.

"Who?"

"Sybilla Triast-Perkins."

"Don't be ridiculous. Sybilla wouldn't hurt a fly."

"She was in the tent before the exhibition was officially open. Her marmalade was one of the ones we know was laced with LSD."

"I was in the tent as well. She did not go near the jam."

"Wait a bit! We're forgetting the tent was empty. They set it up at six in the morning and then went off for breakfast! Anyone in the village could have sneaked in then. I know they had pinned cloths down over the jam, but it would be so easy to lift the cloths and put the LSD into the jam."

"Mrs. Raisin—"

"Agatha, please."

"Agatha. I myself was out at dawn checking all the marquees and making sure they were secure. I hoped you might have some hard news, but all this is the same old speculation."

We forgive beauty such a lot, thought Agatha suddenly. If he was a little balding man with thick glasses, I might get a bit tetchy.

"But this is the way cases are solved!" she said. "You talk and talk and turn it over. The main clues are often in the characters of the suspects. What about Trixie?"

He threw back his head and laughed. "Trixie! Really, Agatha. That is just too far-fetched."

"Why?" demanded Agatha stubbornly.

"Because she is a charming lady and the vicar's wife."

He looked quite cross, so Agatha hurried on. "What about the organizers? Mrs. Glarely and Mrs. Cranton?"

"Innocent ladies. Do a lot of good work in the village. Nothing sinister there."

Agatha sighed. "Can you think of anyone at all?"

"Somehow, I think it must be one of the outsiders."

"But none of the visitors had any opportunity."

"They may have."

"The thing I must find out," said Agatha, "is when exactly Mrs. Andrews and Mrs. Jessop sampled the jam. My assistant, Toni, tried to talk to the organizers, but their husbands chased her off. Now if you were to ask them . . . ?"

He suddenly smiled. Agatha blinked at him, dazzled.

"There's no time like the present. Why don't we drive over there and I'll see what I can do."

Agatha felt elated as they drove off in George's BMW. As his car purred through the Cotswold lanes, she felt the countryside had never looked more beautiful.

At Comfrey Magna, George drove straight along the main street and parked outside Mrs. Cranton's home. Mr. Cranton answered the door. He was a small waspish elderly man. "Evening, Mr. Selby. The missus is right upset."

"I would really like to have a word with her," said George soothingly. "It won't take long. You must see that it's important to find out who did this dreadful thing."

"Okay, but don't spend too long. Her be fair shook up."

Mrs. Cranton was sitting in a stuffy cluttered front parlour, drinking tea and eating biscuits. "Why, Mr. Selby," she said. "How nice of you to call."

"I was worried about you," said George.

A cynical little voice in Agatha's head said, "He can turn that charm of his on and off like a tap."

"This is the detective, Mrs. Raisin. Mr. Chance has employed her to find out who did this dreadful thing. How are you now?"

"Not so bad. I only had a little taste of the awful stuff. I 'member it was Miss Tubby's plum jam. Last year she left stones in it. I said to Doris—that's Mrs. Glarely—let's make sure she hasn't done that again.

We take our jam making seriously in this village, but Miss Tubby and Miss Tolling go on as if it's all a joke. So I tasted a little and then Doris did and then we came over all funny."

"When was this?" asked Agatha.

"Why, it were right before the tent was opened. The vicar and his wife and you, Mr. Selby, and, oh, Miss Triast-Perkins and Mr. Bassett had just left."

"So someone could have crept in while you were off for breakfast?" said Agatha.

"But the marquee was closed. We tied the flap over the entrance."

"Someone could have untied it. I mean, was anyone else about so early?"

"I saw Mr. Selby here. Then Miss Corrie was setting up the tombola stand. Let me see . . . no, can't remember anyone else."

"We won't trouble you any further," said George. "We'll leave you alone."

Mrs. Glarely's husband delivered himself of a tirade against hippies and druggies, leaning on two sticks and glaring at them. George listened carefully and then said, "Of course you are upset. But the sad news is that the jam seems to have been poisoned before any of the visitors arrived."

Mr. Glarely was a tall thin man with an old face

marred by a lifetime of discontent. "S'pose you'd better talk to the wife," he said reluctantly.

Another front parlour. Mrs. Glarely was drinking a clear liquid, which, from the smell, Agatha judged to be neat gin. She gave them a bleary glance. She looked like a twin of Mrs. Cranton—grey hair, tightly permed, wrinkled face, pale eyes.

George explained what they had learned from her friend and then asked, "So when you were both leaving after setting up the exhibits, did you see anyone about?"

But Mrs. Glarely had only seen Miss Corrie at the tombola stand.

"I suppose we'd better call on Fred Corrie," said George when they left the Glarelys' cottage.

"I thought she was a Miss Corrie."

"Oh, Fred's her name. Short for Frederica. Great sport."

Agatha groaned inwardly. She pictured a sturdy, hearty woman with a tweedy brain. "Just a few doors along," said George.

But the woman who answered the door was elfin, something straight out of *The Lord of the Rings*. She had long silvery straight hair, a sweet face and a perfect figure shown off to advantage in a clinging dress of white Indian muslin.

She stood on tiptoe and kissed George on the cheek. "Do come in. Who is this?"

George introduced Agatha. Fred led them through

her cottage to where a large conservatory had been built on the back. It was furnished with cane-backed chairs and sofas with plump cushions. A few exotic-looking plants rose up out of ceramic pots.

It was very quiet except for the evening song of a blackbird perched on a lilac tree in the garden outside.

"I wonder if you can help us," said George. "Mrs. Raisin here is trying to find out who doctored the jam. You were up very early setting up the tombola stand. Did you see anyone?"

"I saw those two ladies, Mrs. Cranton and Mrs. Glarely, leaving the marquee. I wasn't really paying much attention. I had had a restless night, so I got up early to put out the goods and then decided to go back to bed and try to get some sleep."

"Weren't you frightened someone would pinch some of the prizes?" asked Agatha.

Fred gave a tinkling laugh. "No, it's always the same old rubbish except for a bottle of whisky and a bottle of gin and I didn't leave them out. And nobody was going to run off with the tombola wheel. Once the visitors started to pour in, I sold tickets very quickly, turned the wheel and I managed to get rid of everything, even that tin of sardines in tomato sauce that turns up every year."

"Maybe if you could think about the early-morning

bit again," said Agatha. "You saw the two organizers leaving the tent and walking off home. After that, did you even hear anything?"

"Only a cat yowling. I thought there was some animal in pain. It was coming from the churchyard. So I went over and searched, but I couldn't find the animal."

"So someone could have slipped into the tent while you were away," said Agatha eagerly. "Did you try the jam yourself?"

"No, I was too busy turning the wheel and getting rid of the usual old dreck."

Agatha's stomach rumbled. She looked hopefully at George. "Gosh, I'm hungry."

"So am I," said Fred, "and I don't feel like cooking. Let's all go to the pub and get something."

Agatha groaned inwardly. Gone were her hopes of a dinner date alone with George.

The small pub only had two customers when they walked into the low-ceilinged barroom.

"What have you got on the menu tonight, Bruce?" asked Fred.

"Wasn't expecting folks, but I've got a rare bit of ham. You could have that with an egg and chips."

"Great," said Fred. "We'll have three of those."

Agatha wanted to say pettishly that she would select her own food, but, then, there didn't seem to be anything else on offer.

They collected their drinks and sat at a round table which was scarred and stained with years of use. To Agatha's delight, there was a large glass ashtray in front of her.

With a sigh of relief, she pulled out a packet of Benson & Hedges.

"You're never going to smoke!" exclaimed Fred.

Agatha lit up and sighed with pleasure. "Too right, I am."

"Well, I'll be relieved when the smoking ban comes into force," said Fred. "Do you not worry about passive smoking, because I do."

"The pub door is open," said Agatha. "Fresh air is whizzing all around us. I notice a Range Rover parked outside your cottage. Your carbon footprint is a whopping great size twelve. Mine is only a toe mark."

"Has anyone ever told you that you are a very rude woman?" said Fred.

"Maybe. But no one has ever accused me of interfering with anyone's liberty. Oh, belt up, do. I know what the trouble is. Did you used to smoke?"

"Yes, but—"

"Thought so," said Agatha gloomily. "You lot are like converted Catholics. I'm not having any fun any more, so you're not going to have any either. Take this global-warming scam. They say we are taxing your hide off to save the planet. Bollocks! It all goes into that black hole called the Treasury and disappears forever and bugger-all is done to save the earth."

To Agatha's horror, large tears appeared in Fred's eyes and rolled with crystal purity down her cheeks.

"Now look what you've done," said George angrily. He put a comforting arm around Fred's shoulders and handed her a clean handkerchief.

"I c-can't s-stand angry voices," hiccupped Fred.

"Sorry," said Agatha gruffly. "Got a bit carried away."

"I f-forgive you." Fred dabbed at her eyes, but as she lowered the handkerchief, Agatha caught a look of steely venom before she smiled and said, "Silly little me."

"There, now," said George. "No one could call you silly."

The food arrived. Fred talked animatedly to George about people Agatha did not know. The pair seemed to have forgotten her existence.

At least she would have George to herself when he ran her home. Her mind drifted off. She would invite him in for a drink. Perhaps light the logs in the fire. Soft lights. She would be comforting. Get him to talk about his wife. Sit next to him on the sofa and hold his hand, and . . .

"Oh dear, what's the matter, George? Are you getting one of your migraines?"

"I think I've got one coming on," said George, "but I've got to run Agatha home."

"I'll do that," said Fred. "Off you go and take your pills."

At that moment, Charles sauntered into the pub. "Hi, Aggie."

"Oh, Charles," said Agatha with relief. "Can you run me home? George here has a migraine coming on."

"What about a drink first?"

"We'll get one at my place."

"Aren't you going to introduce me?"

Agatha made hurried introductions. Charles smiled at Fred but was soon hustled out of the pub by Agatha.

"What did you do to upset that fair maiden? Her eyes were red," said Charles as he drove off.

"She was complaining about me wanting to smoke."

Charles grinned. "And you blasted her?"

"Not quite. There was no reason for her to start to cry. You know, I am sure that one can cry at will. Nasty little actress. Also, she was around setting up the dreary tombola stand at dawn before the fête got started. She could easily have sneaked into the tent and put LSD in the jam."

"You're jealous. You are ruthlessly pursuing George and I bet you don't even know the first thing about him."

"Talk about something else," growled Agatha.

"Okay. Don't you think it's possible that one of the young people at the show doctored the jam?"

"No. They weren't interested in any of the exhibits. They all came to hear Betsy. Trust me. It was one of the locals. Anyway, I've proof the jam was doctored before the fête opened. I've taken on a new detective, Jimmy Wilson. He's supposed to have good contacts with the police. I'll ask him to find out if the police know how many were affected with the LSD and who they are. Apart from a few young people who might have got some of the stuff after the word went around, I think we'll find it was the locals who suffered. Apart from the women who contributed the jam and one pig farmer who loves the stuff and the lady of the manor, I really don't think anyone else in the village was much interested. It's more of a hamlet than a village, and I think most of them had something on display at one of the other tents."

Disappointed and feeling silly over her pursuit of George, Agatha decided to concentrate on work the next day. She gave instructions to Jimmy Wilson to find out who had been affected by the drugged jam. Then she settled down to work on other cases until some of the fuss had died down.

The following day, Jimmy came in with his report. He said, "The police cleared the tent when they heard about the possibility of drugs. They said only six teenagers managed to get hold of seemed to be a bit spaced out. The forensic reports on the jam are not yet in because, despite what you see on TV, it takes ages. But it seems that both Mrs. Jessop and Mrs. Andrews each had a good taste of Miss Tubby's plum jam. They think there might have been more in that dish than in any of the others, or even that only a few of the dishes might have been drugged."

"Surely they can find that out quickly," complained Agatha. "It's a simple test. Doesn't need a DNA expert."

"Well, it may do," said Jimmy, "if they want to find out who handled the dish."

Agatha groaned. She began to have an uneasy feeling that this might be the one case she could not solve. She would not admit to herself that her defeatist feelings were because she now felt a fool for having so blatantly pursued George.

That evening, Toni braced herself to clear up matters with Bill. He wanted her to come to his home for dinner, but Toni said she would rather have a quiet drink in a pub because there was something personal they needed to discuss.

Bill met her, looking wary. His previous girlfriends, the few that had been straight with him before dumping him, had always said seriously that they wanted to discuss something personal.

After he had bought them drinks, he said wearily, "Out with it. We'll always be friends, and yakkety-yak."

"It's just that I don't love you—meaning, I'm not in love with you," said Toni bravely, "and what's more, you're not in love with me."

"That's not true!" protested Bill. "Mum and Dad were so pleased. Dad was even going to find a house for us . . ."

His voice trailed away before the startled expression on Toni's face.

"Look, Bill," she said gently, "you can't marry someone just because your parents like them. And any girl you turn out to be really in love with won't want your parents butting in to choose where you are going to live once you are married. We've never even been to bed together. And that's because neither of us has been carried away by passion."

"What do you know about passion?" asked Bill sulkily.

"Nothing. But I'd like to. Think about it, Bill. You must have come across someone at some time you felt you couldn't live without."

Bill sat in silence, remembering at least two girls he had yearned after, dreamed about, but somehow, after he had taken them home, romance had died.

"You've been trying to suit your parents," Toni went on. "Next time, try to find someone you want and don't take the girl home until after you've got the ring on her finger."

"I love my parents," said Bill.

"And I envy you that," said Toni. "At least you know who your father is. My mum will never tell me about my father and sometimes I even wonder whether she knows herself."

"Is she still sober?"

"Yes, and doing very well."

"Well, that's that," said Bill. "I mean—us."

"I know you don't want to hear about the friends bit," said Toni. "But honestly, I think we were really meant to be friends."

Bill gave a reluctant smile. "Sometimes, Toni, you seem older than Agatha."

Chapter Four

AT THE END of the following working day, Toni was filing her notes on a case, glad it was over. Because of previous successes, she was often given work for women who wanted to make sure their husbands were not having affairs.

Jimmy Wilson strolled in. "Evening, babes," he said. "Fancy a pint?"

"No, thanks," said Toni. "Not tonight." Jimmy was chubby and somehow he seemed to fill the small office with an oppressive, sweaty presence. Toni had already decided she did not like him. Phil Marshall was a gentleman. Patrick Mulligan looked and behaved like the hard-working copper he used to be, but there was something unhealthy about Jimmy. Toni wondered why he had taken early retirement. It was supposed to be because he had contracted cancer, but she felt sure, somehow, it had been because of some other reason. She moved towards the door. He barred her way.

"C'mon," he said. "Just one drink."

The door behind him swung open, banging into his back. He stepped aside as Agatha strode in, her bearlike eyes darting from Toni's embarrassed face to Jimmy's grinning one.

"I'm just off," said Toni.

"Coming with you." Jimmy moved to take her arm.

"Run along, Toni," said Agatha. "You. Jimmy. Stay."

When Toni had left, Agatha said, "What was all that about?"

"About what?"

"She looked nervous and embarrassed. You were blocking her way."

"I only asked her for a drink."

"Look here. That girl is eighteen and you are too old. If I catch you bothering her again, you're out. Get it! Now sit down and tell me if you've found out anything else."

"Nothing. You told me to leave it for a bit."

"Well, get back on it tomorrow. Good night!"

Toni hurried along in the direction of her flat. She saw a group of her friends, all dressed up, heading in her direction. "Hi, Toni," said Sandra, who was in the lead. "We're off to that new disco, Naughty Nights, out on the Evesham road. Come with us."

Toni had a sudden mental picture of Bill's sad face, followed by one of the leering Jimmy Wilson. She wanted to feel as young as she was, and free.

"I'm not dressed," she said.

"Go home and change and join us," said Sandra.

"I might do that."

At that moment, Wilkes was summoning Bill Wong. "There's a new disco, Naughty Nights, and we want to make sure there's no under-age drinking or drugs. I want you to go there in suitable clothes this evening."

Bill reflected miserably that he had nothing better to do. He went home and changed into black trousers, a black T-shirt and a black leather jacket. As he was getting ready to leave, his father shuffled in, wearing his usual outfit of carpet slippers, open-necked shirt, baggy trousers and a ratty cardigan. The only thing Asian-looking about him was his almond-shaped eyes. The rest was pure British. "Why you going out dressed like a freak?" he asked "Where's that nice suit we bought you for Christmas?"

"Going undercover," said Bill.

His mother joined them. "Have you got a clean hanky?"

"Yes, Mum."

"And clean underwear? What if you was to end up in hospital?"

"I'm fine."

Bill escaped and drove to the nightclub. Before he even reached it, he could hear the *thud, thud, thud* of the disco. When he parked his car and climbed out, the very ground beneath his feet seemed to vibrate to the noise.

Toni was enjoying herself, dancing under the flashing strobe lights, losing herself in the deafening music. Her partner was a thin youth with greasy hair and a face scarred by acne. But he danced like John Travolta in *Grease*. When the music finished, he said, "Want a drink?"

"Okay, I'm thirsty," said Toni.

They shouldered their way through to the bar.

"What'll it be?"

"Just a half of lager."

When the drinks were served, he shouted above the noise, "Look at that weird bird over there!"

Toni swung round. "Which bird?"

"You can't see her now. Drink up."

Toni drank thirstily. Then she began to feel dizzy. "I'd better get outside," she said weakly.

"I'll help you."

Bill was just entering the club when he saw Toni, supported by a young man. Toni looked barely conscious.

"What's happened?" he demanded.

"She's a bit faint. Getting her outside."

"She's a friend of mine. I'll take over."

"Get lost, mate."

Bill flashed his badge. The youth stopped supporting

Toni, who fell to the floor. The youth turned to flee. Bill seized him by his denim jacket, forced him to his knees, and handcuffed him to the leg of a desk by the door.

Then he phoned for backup and for an ambulance.

Agatha arrived at Mircester Hospital with Charles later that evening, having been phoned by Bill. Bill was waiting for them outside the ward where Toni was stretched out on one of the beds.

"What happened?" asked Agatha.

"We think someone slipped a date-rape drug into her drink," said Bill. "The hospital's taken tests. It was all Wilkes needed as an excuse to raid the club. They were selling a combination of Viagra and Ecstasy. No wonder there are so many rapes these days."

"Why did Toni go to such a place?" cried Agatha.

"She's young," said Charles. "Young people go to discos. Here's her mother."

Mrs. Gilmour arrived looking harried and distressed, followed by a doctor. She nodded to Agatha and was taken into the ward where Toni lay.

They waited impatiently. At last the doctor emerged. "Mrs. Gilmour is going to stay with her daughter, but there is nothing to worry about. The girl will be all right in the morning."

"Cheer up," said Charles, and he and Agatha walked away. "This time it's not your fault."

"I worry about her," said Agatha. "I wish she weren't so young. I mean, if something happened to Phil, say, it would be pretty awful, but he is in his seventies and he's had a long life. But poor Toni is really just starting out."

"It must be difficult for one so young being in an office full of old people," commented Charles as they emerged from the hospital.

"Watch it," said Agatha furiously. "I am *not* old."

Charles stifled a yawn. "I'd better get off back home. Things to do."

Agatha felt bereft. There were times when she was furious at the way he used her cottage like a hotel, but now that she was no longer interested in George and there was no reason to wish him out of the way, she reluctantly admitted to herself that she would miss Charles's company.

So Agatha was relieved on returning home to find a message on her phone from Roy Silver, her former employee, asking if he could come down for the weekend.

Agatha phoned him and said she would be delighted to see him with more warmth in her voice than Roy had heard before.

"You might have asked me to that murderous gig," said Roy petulantly.

"Honestly, Roy, with all the flurry of last-minute arrangements, I forgot. I'm sorry."

There was a little silence while Roy digested the fact that Agatha Raisin was actually apologizing to him.

"I'll be at Moreton-in-Marsh on Friday evening. Train gets in at six-twenty."

"I'll be there," promised Agatha.

Agatha felt guilty at leaving what she thought of as the Jam Case alone, but was looking forward to a lazy weekend with Roy.

When he descended from the train on Friday, she saw he was all dressed in black: black leather jacket, black shirt, black trousers, and black high-heeled boots. He had even dyed his hair black. He pirouetted on the platform.

"Why the Man in Black effect?" asked Agatha.

"Because we'll be going detecting, Aggie."

"Don't call me Aggie, and I want the weekend off."

"You can't just leave it! I'll take you for dinner and you can tell me all about it."

"You can take me to the Black Bear. It's the only place left where I can smoke before this dreadful non-smoking ban hits the country."

Agatha felt her enthusiasm for the case returning as she carefully described what she had found out.

"Fascinating," said Roy, ignoring the fact that some beefy-looking men at the bar were looking across at him and sniggering. "How's Toni getting on?"

Agatha told him about the date-rape drug and finished by saying, "She's back at work and appears none the worse."

"So to get back to your case," said Roy, "you said most of the LSD might have been in the jam supplied by Miss Tubby. So we start there. Let's go and see her tomorrow."

"You'd better wear something more conservative. She and her partner are a couple of bitches."

"I think I look rather smart in a sinister way."

Agatha looked at Roy's rather weak face topped with its crop of gelled dyed-black hair. "Very nice for London," said Agatha with rare tact. "But a bit too exotic for down here."

Agatha felt a twinge of reluctance as they approached the village on the following day. The police unit was still in evidence, but apart from that, the village seemed to have sunk back into its usual rural torpor.

"We'll call at the vicarage first," said Agatha. "I'm employed by the vicar to solve this case."

"Must we?" complained Roy. "I don't like holy people."

"You like Mrs. Bloxby."

"That's different. Everyone likes Mrs. Bloxby."

The door was opened by Trixie. She was wearing a white-lace vintage morning dress. Agatha's expert eye, honed by working in the past for various couture houses, estimated it was genuine and must have cost a mint.

"Lovely dress," said Agatha. "Your husband at home?"

"Yes, go through to the garden."

They followed her. Trixie's blonde hair flowed down her back. She's really rather sexy in a feral way, thought Agatha. Without that dress and hair, she wouldn't get far in the attraction stakes with her mean features.

The vicar was seated at a garden table under the shade of a cedar tree with the accountant, Arnold Birntweather. Mr. Chance looked up and saw Agatha. The sun flashed on his thick glasses as Agatha and Roy approached, giving him a blind look.

"Welcome!" he cried. "We're just going over the accounts."

Agatha introduced Roy. "Sit down," urged the vicar. "We are just deciding who gets what out of the money. We cannot take it all for the church when there are so many needy charities."

Trixie appeared, carrying a tray with a jug of lemonade and glasses.

Agatha said, "I forgot to introduce Roy to you, Trixie. This is a friend of mine, Roy Silver."

Trixie cast Roy an amused look. Agatha could only be glad that Roy had changed into a conservative shirt and trousers. She had already put Trixie down as a bitch.

Trixie set down the tray and then put an arm around Arnold's bent shoulders. "Stop fussing over the accounts on such a lovely day," she cooed.

Arnold smiled but said, "They've got to be done."

"Oh, nonsense, have some lemonade."

Arnold let out a cry as Trixie poured lemonade over the account papers.

"I'm so very sorry," said Trixie. "Here. I'll take them away and dry them."

Agatha noticed a washing line at the end of the garden. "We could peg them up on the washing line," she said. "They'd be dry in no time. Has the writing been washed away?"

"No, it's still quite clear," said Arnold.

"Come along. I'll help you," said Agatha. "No, don't anyone else bother. I'm an expert at this sort of thing."

She carried the spoiled papers down to the end of the garden and carefully pinned them up, her mind working furiously. Trixie is wearing an expensive dress. She did that deliberately. Trixie must have been stealing from the funds.

"Where is the money kept, Arnold?" she asked.

"In the vicarage."

"I think you should take it yourself and put it in a safe deposit box in the bank. Think about it. Someone who has committed murder wouldn't stop short at a robbery."

The vicar came to join them. "My poor wife begs to be excused. She is very distressed."

"It's all right," said Arnold. "Thanks to Mrs. Raisin's idea, there is no harm done."

"Please call me Agatha."

"Very well. Agatha. Although I find this modern

business of calling acquaintances by their first names very . . . familiar. Agatha has had a splendid idea."

He outlined the idea for putting all the money in a safe deposit box.

"Excellent," enthused the vicar. "It certainly is not safe to keep so much money at the vicarage. I'll go and bag it up. Perhaps we can each have a key to the box, Arnold?"

"Just for yourself and Arnold," said Agatha quickly. "No one else."

"Of course."

There was no sign of Trixie when they entered the vicarage. The money was packed into bags. Then Agatha and Roy escorted Arnold to his bank and waited while he made arrangements for the safe deposit box and saw the money safely stowed away. "I forgot that Mr. Chance should have come with us to sign for the other key," said Arnold as they left the bank.

Back in the village, they refused Arnold's invitation to join him for tea in his cottage.

Agatha had parked the car near the church. "We'll walk from here," she said. "Must get some exercise."

"So what was that all about?" asked Roy. "Don't you trust the vicar?"

"I don't trust his wife. First, that gown she was wearing cost a fortune. Secondly, she deliberately spilled lemonade over the accounts. Thirdly, I think she's getting her harpy fingers into the money."

"But what about that poor accountant? What if someone forces him to get the money and then bumps him off?"

Agatha stood stock-still. Then she said, "Snakes and bastards. I might be risking his life. Back to Arnold's we go."

Agatha explained carefully to Arnold that he should give her the key and let it be known that she had it. The elderly accountant looked relieved. "I do feel all that money is a great responsibility. The manager at the bank was very helpful. He said I could use a little room there to do the accounts and that means the money does not need to leave the bank. Then when I have counted it thoroughly—I thought I had already done so, but there seem to be some discrepancies—it can go into a separate account and then cheques can be sent to the various beneficiaries."

"You mean, money is missing?"

"Oh, I am sure it is all down to my faulty eyesight. Here is the key. I will collect it from you when I need it at your office if you will supply me with the address."

Agatha handed him a card. "I'll go with you," she said. "When it gets to the chequebook stage, there is no reason for anyone else to have to sign the cheques."

"I had thought of two signatures, mine and Mr. Chance."

"I don't think that will be necessary," said Agatha briskly.

"Now you've put your own life at risk," said Roy as they walked back to their original parking place.

"I think I've made it all too complicated for dear Trixie."

"What if it's someone else?"

"There is no one else. Oh, here comes the lady of the manor."

Miss Triast-Perkins came slowly towards them. "Have you just come from the vicarage?" she asked.

"We were there earlier," said Agatha.

"Was Mrs. Chance wearing a lace gown?"

"Yes, she was."

"Now that is too bad of her. That was one of my grandmother's gowns. I lent it to her for amateur the-atricals, to be worn carefully onstage but not around the house. I shall go and get it back now. I should never have lent it to her."

Miss Triast-Perkins tottered off on a pair on unsuit-able high-heeled sandals.

"Now, what have I done?" said Agatha gloomily.

"Maybe it's the vicar."

"Maybe it's just Arnold's eyesight," said Agatha. "I should have gone over the books with him. I wonder if those papers have been collected off the washing line, or Trixie's found some way to destroy them."

"You've really got your knife into the vicar's wife. Why?"

Agatha shrugged. "I can't help feeling she deliberately poured lemonade over those papers."

"Well, let's call at the vicarage and find out."

At the vicarage, Arthur Chance greeted them with surprise, and to their questions he answered that, yes, the papers had dried quickly and George Selby had just left to take them to the accountant.

"So there you are," said Roy cheerfully as they walked back through the village. "Who's George Selby?"

"Just one of the parishioners. Here we are. Brace yourself to meet Maggie Tubby and Phyllis Tolling."

Phyllis answered the door. "Oh, it's you again," she said. "Who's this? The office boy?"

"Roy Silver is a friend of mine," snapped Agatha. "We want to talk to Maggie."

"Come in and get it over with. She's in her shed in the garden."

They followed her through the cottage into the garden and to a large shed at the end. The door was open and Maggie could be seen working at a potter's wheel. When she saw them, Maggie switched off the wheel, leaving an as yet unshaped lump of clay on it.

She looked amused. "What now?"

"It appears as if your plum jam had the most LSD in it," said Agatha.

"These are gorgeous," exclaimed Roy, examining a bench laden with coffee cups, bowls and vases, all in beautiful coloured glazes. "You could sell them at the top shops in London."

"I already do," said Maggie.

"Really? How much is this bowl?"

"About two hundred pounds."

"Blimey," said Roy. "You should have a flat in Kensington instead of living in this poky cottage."

"We are perfectly happy living in this village, thank you. Or rather, we were before a serpent called Agatha Raisin came into our lives."

Agatha said loudly, "Can we get to the point? Why had your jam got such a lot of the drug in it?"

"Blessed if I know. Maybe it was the first to hand. I mean, if someone was trying to drug people, they wouldn't be too careful about delicately measuring out the drops. Now would they?"

All Agatha's resentment and dislike of Trixie switched to these two women. She suddenly wished the murderer would turn out to be one of them, or both. She felt like throwing some sort of bomb into what she damned as their smug, patronizing lives.

Phyllis, who had been standing behind Agatha, said, "Perhaps you should go back to murder number one."

Agatha swung round. "Mrs. Andrews?"

"No, Sarah Selby."

"Why her?"

"Well, dear George was in need of funds, Sarah Selby was heavily insured. Sybilla Triast-Perkins was besotted with George. Work it out."

"I don't think it has anything to do with this case," said Agatha.

"Why?"

"Mr. George Selby seems genuinely to be grieving the death of his wife."

"That's what he would like everyone to think."

Agatha was exasperated. "Have you any proof?"

"Just intuition. I am not dazzled by George's green eyes the way you seem to be."

"I am a hard-working detective. I am not dazzled by anyone. I've been trying to find out why Maggie's jam sample seems to have contained the most of the drug."

"Then find out who did it and you'll get your answer. Please leave."

Toni was at that moment walking slowly home, feeling that at her age she ought to have a date for Saturday evening.

She heard herself being hailed and swung round. Harry Beam, Agatha's former young detective, came running up to meet her. "How are things?" he asked.

"I suppose they're pretty much what they were when you were working for Agatha," said Toni, "except for the village drugging case."

"I'd like to hear about that. Got time for a drink?"

"Sure. There's a pub over there. But it'll be noisy. I tell you what, come up to my place. We could buy some beer at the corner shop."

Soon they were ensconced in Toni's flat. After throwing out the shabby bits of furniture that had come with the flat, Toni had set about buying her own. It was a pleasant mixture of cheap assemble-it-yourself pieces and two Victorian and Edwardian ones that Toni had picked up at junk shops. A Victorian wide-seated chair was covered in chintz to disguise the fact that it had only three legs, with a sawed-down broom handle making up the missing fourth. The Edwardian bureau had water damage but had been polished to a high shine to hide its deficiencies. The only new item was a small two-seater sofa, sold cheap because it was in a brilliant shade of purple.

"This is nice," said Harry, looking around.

"Agatha found the flat for me. She's awfully generous."

"You must be a very good detective," said Harry cynically. "She's just protecting her assets. She probably hopes you'll be so grateful, you'll never leave. Do you live rent-free?"

"No, she bought it for me, but I'm paying her rent each month."

Harry was casually but expensively dressed. He had stopped shaving his head and wearing studs and earrings. Toni noticed that the jacket he had taken off and slung over the back of the sofa was of fine soft suede and his sweater cashmere.

He was tall with a strong pleasant face.

"I never really got a chance to talk to you at Agatha's Christmas party," said Toni, handing him a bottle of beer. "Has the university term finished?"

"Not yet. I'm home for the weekend to see my parents. Tell me about this village case."

Toni succinctly told him everything they had found out so far.

Harry seized on one fact when Toni had finished. "You mean to say Agatha's got the key to the strongbox?"

"So she says."

"That's dangerous."

"Do you think so? I think the money will be quite safe. I think some loony put LSD in the jam and won't try anything again."

"Look here. I'd like to see this village. I've got my bike parked in the square. Why don't we take a trip over?"

"All right," said Toni. "Maybe we'll find out something."

Chapter Five

TONI ENJOYED HER RIDE on the back of Harry's motorbike. He parked beside the churchyard wall.

"That was ace," cried Toni, removing her helmet and handing it to Harry.

"It's a good way of getting around Cambridge," said Harry. "The traffic can be awful. Goodness, it's quiet here. You'd never think it was a Saturday."

The cobbled village street led down from the church-yard, the cottages on either side leaning towards the road, like so many elderly people, looking for support. Somewhere up on the hills surrounding the village came the sound of a tractor. A dog barked from the other end of the street. But all those sounds seemed to do was intensify the silence. It was very hot despite a little breeze.

"Where do you want to start?" asked Toni. She turned round and saw Agatha's car. She suddenly did not want her day with Harry to be spoiled by encountering Agatha.

"I know," she said quickly. "Back on the bike. There's

this pig farmer, Hal Bassett. He likes me. I think there's a lot more he can tell us. It's straight down the main street and up the hill."

"Isn't that Agatha?"

"Don't let her see us," urged Toni. "Bassett doesn't like her and he won't talk freely."

They put their helmets on and raced off down the village street. "Morons," grumbled Agatha as they roared past, not recognizing either Toni or Harry in their helmets.

The farmer seemed delighted to see Toni again. "The wife's over in Mircester," he said. "Who's this?"

"Harry Beam," said Toni.

"This your fellow?"

"Harry used to work for Agatha Raisin. He's now studying at Cambridge," explained Toni.

"Got away from the old bat, did you? You should do the same, Toni."

Toni was about to flare up in Agatha's defence but stopped herself just in time. Arguing with Hal wouldn't elicit any information.

"Come into the house," he said. "And we'll have some tea, unless you would like something stronger."

"Tea's fine."

They followed him into the kitchen. Harry looked around. "Your kitchen's cool," he said.

"It's the stone flags and the thick walls that keeps it

that way," said Hal, not recognizing the slang. "Sit down. What brings you?"

Toni remembered studying Agatha's notes on the case. Hal had his back to them as he plugged in the electric kettle.

"I wondered if you had thought about what happened at the fête and come up with any ideas," said Toni.

"Are you sure it wasn't one of the visitors?"

"I've got a feeling it was someone in the village."

"Then it must have been someone mad. And if you want someone mad, try Sybilla Triast-Perkins."

"Why her?"

"I think she had her head turned when she fell in love with George Selby. It wouldn't surprise me to learn that she pushed Mrs. Selby downstairs. Now, George has got his eye on the vicar's wife, folk say. So jealous Sybilla could have poisoned the jam in the hope that Trixie got some of it. Now, here's the tea. Don't use sugar or milk. This is white tea."

"You should just have given us ordinary tea," protested Harry. "That stuff is very expensive."

"What is white tea?" asked Toni.

"It comes from the same plant as green tea," said Hal, "but the leaves are picked and harvested before the leaves open fully. This is Silver Needle. Best way is to let it infuse in water just below boiling point. Little caffeine and full of antioxidants."

Toni sipped her cupful cautiously. It tasted light and sweet and was very refreshing.

"Now, as I was saying . . ." Hal was just beginning when his wife strode into the kitchen.

She went straight up to the table, lifted the lid of the teapot and sniffed. She turned a furious face on her husband. "What the hell are you doing serving *my* white tea to this lot?"

"It's my money that pays for it," shouted the farmer.

Toni and Harry got to their feet and began to edge towards the door. Mrs. Bassett glared at Toni. "You're that little snoop. Get out of my house!"

Outside, they hurriedly put on their helmets and climbed on the bike just as a teapot came sailing through the open kitchen window and shattered at their feet.

Harry revved up and they raced off. He stopped again at the churchyard wall. "Whew," he said, as they took off their helmets again, "I'd hate to be married to Mrs. Bassett. Let's have a look at the church."

"Why?"

"I like looking at old churches."

They walked into the dark quiet of Saint Odo The Severe. "It must have been a Saxon church at one time," said Harry. "The pews are quite modern. Do you know, Toni, that before Tudor times, there weren't any seats? People had to stand. But by the reign of Elizabeth the First, sermons had got longer and longer, sometimes four hours, so they had to start letting people sit down. There would have been a rood screen between the chancel and the nave, but I'll bet Cromwell's soldiers hacked it down."

Toni felt very alone. Harry was from another world. In her world, people didn't go to church or even think of enthusing about church architecture. Harry had the ease of manner which obviously came from a comfortable background. Why couldn't I have fancied Bill? wondered Toni. I never felt out of place with Bill.

Agatha and Roy drove to the manor house, parked outside, and stood for a moment, Agatha wondering what she should say to Sybilla. Her usual method of detective work was to ask people question after question, like shaking a tree, in the hope that some piece of valuable information would come loose.

The air was very still and hot. Not a leaf on the trees moved. It was as if the whole countryside were waiting for something.

Roy looked up at the cloudless sky and said, "Going to be a storm soon."

"What do you know about anything?" demanded Agatha huffily. She now prided herself on being a countrywoman.

Roy shrugged his thin shoulders. "I feel it coming."

"You shouldn't wear hair gel in this heat," said Agatha. "It's melting and you've got a snail trail of gel down one cheek."

Roy squawked in dismay and scrubbed at his face with a handkerchief. Agatha rang the bell.

Following the shrill ring of the bell, silence descended once more.

"Must be out," said Roy.

"Maybe she's in the garden and didn't hear the bell. Let's walk round the back."

Agatha pushed open a wrought-iron gate at the side of the manor and, followed by Roy, walked along a weedy path and round into the garden at the back. There were a few signs to show that it had once been a large and beautiful garden. A central path framed by a few struggling rose bushes led to a dry fountain where dusty marble dolphins cavorted over a wide marble basin. Weeds now choked the flower beds.

Agatha walked up shallow steps to a long terrace. "One of the French windows is open," she said. "Come along, Roy."

"We can't just walk in," said Roy.

"We'll call out. Mrs. Triast-Perkins!" yelled Agatha. Silence.

"Let's get out of here," hissed Roy.

Agatha walked in through the open French window and found herself in the over-furnished drawing room where she had previously talked to Sybilla.

Roy hovered just inside, prepared to flee.

Agatha walked through the long drawing room and out into the hall. Perhaps Sybilla was taking an afternoon nap. She stood at the bottom of the curved eighteenth-century staircase and decided that they had better leave. Sybilla probably often left that window open, dating as she did from the days when it was safe to do so.

Agatha half turned away and stumbled over a high-heeled shoe lying on the floor. She picked it up and looked upwards and let out a cry of shock.

Sybilla was hanging by the neck from the rail of the balcony on the first floor. Her face was distorted. She was wearing only one shoe.

Agatha dropped the shoe she was holding and hurried out to join Roy. "She's dead," she gasped.

"Murder?"

"Looks like suicide. Outside now, while I call the police."

Toni and Harry emerged from the gloom of the church and stood blinking in the sunlight. Police cars were racing past and police and detectives were tumbling out of the mobile police unit. Villagers were standing outside their doors.

The vicar came panting up. "What's happened?" he asked.

"I don't know."

"That's the manor house they're going to," said Arthur Chance.

Toni and Harry followed the vicar up to the manor house. But a policeman was already on guard at the gate and they were not allowed to pass.

"That's Agatha's car parked outside," said Toni, looking up the drive. "I hope she's all right."

Roy and Agatha sat on the stone steps of the terrace. They had been told not to move until the police were ready for them.

Agatha puffed at a cigarette.

"What are you going to do when the smoking ban comes in July?" asked Roy.

"Smoke, of course. Unless the bastards bring in a law that says you can't smoke in your own home."

"But the countryside's such a healthy place."

"No, it's not. I just read that a farting cow produces more damage to the ozone layer that a four-wheel-drive. Oh, here's Wilkes, but without Collins. I hope she's finally left. Bill said she was going to Scotland Yard."

"Right, Mrs. Raisin," said Wilkes. "While the forensic team are busy, I want you to come to the police unit and make a statement."

Agatha saw Toni's anxious face as she drove past.

"That was Harry Beam with Toni," said Agatha. "I wonder what he's doing here?"

"I wish I could wash and brush up," said Roy.

"Why?"

"There will be press here shortly."

"I think the police will keep this quiet as long as possible. Wait a minute! When you said you were going down the garden for a pee, did you phone anyone?"

"What do you take me for?"

"I take you for someone who loves getting his picture in the papers."

"Agatha! Really!" Roy suddenly felt his mobile phone burning a hole in his pocket. Would the police check it? Would they find out he had phoned two of the nationals? He eased it out of his pocket and let it slide to the floor of the car.

When they got out of the car, Roy looked up at the sky. "There you are. I knew a storm was coming."

Great black clouds were building up to the west.

They got out of the car. "You first, Mrs. Raisin," said Wilkes.

The inside of the police unit was like an oven.

Wilkes left the door open and switched on an electric fan. Bill Wong was there. He put a tape in the recorder, stated the time, day, and who was interviewing whom, and the questioning started.

Agatha was beginning to suffer from delayed shock,

so she made just a brief statement of how she had come to discover Sybilla.

"Why did you go to see her?" asked Wilkes.

Agatha hesitated. She had really wanted to know if there was any way in which Sybilla could have killed George's wife, but she didn't want to think about George and had no proof at all, so she said instead, "I just wondered if she had heard any gossip around the village, any feuds or competition in the jam-making business. Stuff like that. Was it suicide? Did she leave a note?"

"Yes. It's a straightforward case of suicide."

"Was the note typewritten?" asked Agatha eagerly.

"This is not *Morse*. This is real life," said Wilkes. "The letter was in her own handwriting as far as we can judge at the moment."

"And what did it say?" asked Agatha.

Wilkes hesitated. He hated giving Agatha any information at all. Then he said reluctantly, "It said, 'I cannot continue to live with a death on my conscience.' And it is signed."

"A death? *One* death? But there were two deaths. Could she have been ref— Never mind."

"But we do mind," put in Bill Wong, his almond-shaped eyes shrewd. "Did you have another death in mind?"

"No, no, I don't know what I meant," said Agatha hurriedly.

The questioning went on. At last she was glad to escape and dragged Roy away from a group of reporters and told him the police were waiting for him.

"Don't say anything about us thinking Sybilla might have murdered George's wife," she hissed.

She gave a succinct statement to the press about how she and Roy had found the body and then hurried to her car. They followed her, but she switched on the engine and turned on the air conditioning until they retreated.

There was a gentle rise outside the churchyard where she was parked and she could see the road dipping down into the village. Huge black clouds were towering up in the sky above the end of the village. Seeing that the press had decided to leave her alone, Agatha opened the windows and switched off the engine.

The sunlight was retreating before the menacing black cliff of clouds. There was a blinding white flash of lightning and then a tremendous clap of thunder. With a great *whoosh* the rain came pouring down. Agatha closed the windows. The rain was so heavy, so monsoon-like, that it was like being parked in the middle of a waterfall.

The passenger door was wrenched open and Roy tumbled in. "I'm soaked," he wailed. "I asked them to let me stay in the unit for a bit until the rain eased off, but they wouldn't let me."

"Let's go home," said Agatha. "There's nothing more we can do here in this storm."

Toni and Harry had run to the church again for shelter. Toni began to feel awkward in his presence. He obviously came from a well-to-do family while her background of a slummy house, drunken mother, brother who had committed suicide and a father she did not know weighed heavily on her.

Harry, seemingly unaware of her discomfort, chatted on about his life at Cambridge.

At last, Toni interrupted him. "I think the storm's rolled over."

They went outside into a yellow, watery sunlight. Everything glittered with raindrops and a golden river ran down the middle of the village street.

They mounted Harry's bike and set off. When they reached her flat, Toni dismounted and said awkwardly, "Thanks for the ride."

"What about this evening?" asked Harry cheerfully. "Fancy a bit of dinner?"

"No. I've got a date," lied Toni.

"Oh. Right. See you around."

Agatha was pacing up and down the living room of her cottage, a gin and tonic in one hand and a cigarette in the other.

"I wonder if Sybilla left everything to George in her will."

"But it seems a clear case of suicide," said Roy.

"Suicides can be faked."

"The note was clear enough. I'm watching *Law &
Order*. We'll talk later."

Agatha glanced at the screen. "The rich kid did it."

"You've seen it before!"

"No, I haven't. American television can be terribly
snobby. If there's a rich college kid, he's always the murderer."

"I want to see it," complained Roy.

Agatha retreated to the kitchen and was just sitting
down at the table when the doorbell rang. She opened
the door and found Bill Wong looking quizzically at
her.

"Come in," said Agatha. "Where's your boss?"

"This is unofficial. You were about to say something.
Why were you surprised that only one death was referred to in the suicide note?"

"I wasn't."

"I know you of old. Out with it. Agatha, you've got
into trouble before and nearly got yourself killed by not
telling me the full story."

Agatha capitulated. "Oh, sit down. Drink?"

"No, I'm driving. Coffee would be nice."

"Right. There's some still hot in the percolator."

When Bill was seated at the table, with Agatha's cats
climbing over him, Agatha began to outline the idea she

had formulated that George Selby's wife had been pushed down the stairs by Sybilla. "Those two jam-making lesbians, Maggie Tubby and Phyllis Tolling, seem pretty sure of it. Mind you, they are a malicious pair of women. But I had the idea that if I could solve that case—assuming there was a case to be solved—then it might lead to whoever poisoned the jam. And if Sybilla was so dotty about George that he suggested she bump off his wife, he might have driven her to suicide, hoping to inherit her money."

"We found Sybilla's will. She had a sister, Cassandra. Cassandra gets the lot. She is a Mrs. Unwin, married well. Husband is head of a building contractors'. Pots of money."

"But George might have *thought* she would leave it all to him."

"I know you've had far-fetched ideas before that turned out to be true, but this one is ridiculous. Also, I don't think the poisoning of the jam was intended to kill anyone. I think it was a senseless prank that went wrong. Think about it. There seems to have been no specific target. That's what was making it so difficult trying to find out who did it. But now we are sure it was Sybilla. There is no other explanation for her suicide or for that note. As far as Wilkes is concerned, the case is closed. He told the vicar his conclusions, so I'm afraid, if you want to go on pursuing the matter, you won't be paid for it."

———

Agatha was increasingly busy in the following weeks and put the Comfrey Magna case out of her mind. She needed to build up a healthy bank balance to make up for all she had spent on the fête. It was suddenly considered fashionable by all sorts of people to hire a private detective. Women wanted to find out if their partners or husbands were cheating on them and were prepared to pay Agatha fifteen hundred pounds each for her agency's skills. Agatha could remember a time when only the rich took foreign holidays in winter. Now loads of ordinary odds and sods crammed the airport departure lounges. Once, a visit to the beautician was for people with money. Now it was a growth industry. Hiring a private detective seemed to be the latest thing to do.

Occasionally, she worried about Toni. The girl seemed to have lost a lot of her sparkle, although her work was as efficient as ever.

One Friday evening when she found herself alone with Toni in the office, Agatha said, "Let's go for dinner."

"All right," said Toni. "Where?"

"There's a new fish restaurant in Mircester, the other side of the square. It's supposed to be good."

Once settled over plates of Dover sole and a carafe of house white, Agatha said, "Out with it."

"With what?"

"There's nothing up with your work, Toni, but you've

been looking depressed and that's not like you. Is it anything to do with Bill?"

No, it's . . ."

"Are you pregnant?"

"Absolutely not!"

"So what's up?"

"It's silly."

"I can be the queen of silliness where men are concerned," said Agatha with a rare burst of honesty.

"It's Harry Beam."

"My Harry Beam? What happened? I saw you both in Comfrey Magna and have been meaning to ask you about that."

Toni told her about meeting Harry in Mircester and about their trip to Comfrey Magna, ending with "He asked me out for dinner, but I said I had a date."

"And you didn't?"

"No."

"Why?"

"You know my background, Agatha. Harry's posh. I felt intimidated."

"Don't be. Nothing to be ashamed of. Your mother's sobered up a treat. You haven't anyone else in your family to worry about."

"It's just . . . I feel caught between two worlds. All my friends are from working-class backgrounds."

"I'll bet your mind raced on to the wedding and to meeting his parents."

Toni gave a reluctant smile. "Something like that."

"I wouldn't worry about the English class system," said Agatha, pouring more wine into their glasses. "People do go on about it, but it's not as bad as France or Spain, say. These days, anyone with a job is now middle class. You'll come across pockets of snobbery in the Gloucestershire middle classes, but those people are not worth bothering about. I had a lousy drunken family background just like you. Harry's the last person to worry about where you come from. When the university holidays start, I'll ask him to dinner with a few other people and you can take it from there. I feel pretty insecure socially at times, but I just charge along regardless. So don't worry. Now, on to another subject. What do you make of Jimmy Wilson?"

"I don't like him," said Toni. "He leers at me and makes my skin crawl. I wonder why he left the police force without waiting for retirement?"

"There's a point. I sometimes wonder if he really did have cancer. I'll get Patrick to ask around. Now, cheer up!"

They drank a lot more wine and followed it up with large brandies. Agatha decided she had better leave her car and take a taxi home.

When the cab turned into Lilac Lane where her cottage was, she was dismayed to see that a police car and a van from the security firm, which had installed her burglar alarm, were parked outside.

A policeman came up to meet her as she got out of the taxi and paid off the driver. "What's happened?" she asked.

"Are you Mrs. Agatha Raisin?"

"Yes, yes. What's going on?"

"Someone tried to break into your house by the kitchen door. The alarm went off. Whoever it was seems to have been frightened by the alarm and ran away without going into the house, but you had better check and see if anything is missing."

Agatha unlocked the front door and went in. "We turned off the alarm," said a security man behind her. "We'll reset it, but you'll need some repairs to your kitchen door."

Alerted by the police activity, villagers began to head towards Agatha's cottage. The local carpenter said he would go back and fetch his tools and fix the door. Agatha turned down various offers of cups of tea.

Bill Wong drove up. "Do you think this was an ordinary burglar, Agatha, or have you been stirring something up in one of your cases?"

Agatha fiddled nervously with a silver chain around her neck and then, with an exclamation, pulled the whole chain out of her blouse to reveal a safe deposit box key attached to the end.

"I wonder if it could have been anything to do with this."

"Tell me about it," said Bill. Mrs. Bloxby came hurrying up, asking what had happened, and Bill waited impatiently while Agatha explained how her cottage had been broken into.

"Agatha was just about to tell me why it might be something to do with the key hanging around her neck. We'd better go somewhere quiet. A forensic team should be arriving shortly."

"We'll go to the vicarage," said Mrs. Bloxby. "My husband is out this evening and no one will disturb you."

In the comfortable peace of the vicarage, Agatha explained how she had kept the safe deposit key in order to protect the accountant.

"Now that the LSD case has been solved, I don't think you need to worry any more."

"I'm not so sure," said Agatha. "It's like this. The terrible twosome, Tubby and Tolling, say that Sybilla pushed George Selby's wife downstairs. What if Sybilla's suicide note was only apologizing for that and the LSD maniac is still at large?"

"What has that got to do with the money?"

"Just a feeling."

"I have an idea," said Mrs. Bloxby. "Mrs. Raisin, leave the key with the police. I will pay a visit to Comfrey Magna tomorrow and let as many people as possible know that that is where the key is."

"Good idea," said Agatha. She lifted the chain with the key from around her neck and handed it to Bill. He wrote out a receipt and gave it to her.

"Now, let it go, Agatha," said Bill. "I checked our records on the death of Sarah Selby and it did seem to be a straightforward accident. She was carrying a tray and lost her balance."

"And yet it took Sybilla Triast-Perkins one whole hour before she phoned the emergency services."

"She said she fainted with shock."

"Oh, yeah?"

"Agatha, I'm sure you've got enough on your hands at that agency of yours without trying to find out murders that never existed. I've got to go."

Toni at that moment was thinking uneasily of Agatha's offer to hold a dinner party so that she could meet Harry again.

With her mother being drunk and incapable until comparatively recently, Toni had brought herself up. Agatha had already organized her life by finding her a flat and buying her a car. Toni suddenly felt she wanted a part of her life that was private and had nothing to do with Agatha. She had her own key to her office. Toni let herself out of her flat and walked round to the agency. Once inside, she searched the computer files until she found Harry's e-mail address.

She decided to write to him. "Dear Harry," she typed. "I am sorry I turned down your invitation for dinner. I didn't have a date. I'm a bit shy, that's all. Hope to see you again. Toni."

She left the computer on, made herself a cup of coffee, and sat down on the sofa to watch the computer screen. After half an hour there was a ping from the computer signalling the arrival of new mail. Eagerly she read it. It said, "Dear Toni. See you next Saturday? OK? Harry."

Hurriedly Toni typed back. "Dear Harry, I'll meet you on Saturday at The George in Mircester. Eight o'clock. OK? Toni."

She waited anxiously. Back came a message. "Great, see you then, Harry."

Toni felt a rush of elation. She carefully deleted all the e-mails to and from Harry. Then she began to worry. What if Harry couldn't make it and e-mailed the office and Agatha read it? She hurriedly typed out another e-mail to him, giving him her mobile phone number and telling him to text or call her if by any chance he couldn't keep the appointment. She sent it off, deleted it and switched off the computer.

Agatha, finally in bed in her cottage and listening nervously to every rustling in the thatch above, decided to delegate all the agency work and return to Comfrey

Magna. Even if someone had meant the LSD to be just a silly joke, two women had died and that meant unsolved murders. She somehow did not believe that Sybilla had been responsible.

Chapter Six

THE WEATHER WAS MISERABLE. Ever since the thunderstorm, it had rained steadily, weeping from heavily laden clouds that seemed to sit on top of the Cotswolds hills.

Agatha's cats, Hodge and Boswell, mewed disconsolately as they stared out at the deluge from the ledge in front of the kitchen window.

Everything felt damp, but the air was not cold; rather it was heavy, hot and humid. Meteorologists said it was the La Niña effect, as opposed to the El Niño, which all seemed to mean that it was guaranteed to rain and rain for weeks to come.

Agatha drove to Comfrey Magna and parked outside the vicarage. She climbed out of her car, unfurled a large umbrella and hurried to the vicarage door, wishing she had worn Wellington boots, for her shoes were soaked by the time she covered the short distance to the shelter of the front porch.

Trixie answered the door, her golden hair cascading about her shoulders. "So what now?" she asked rudely.

"I would like to have a word with your husband," said Agatha.

"If you must. Come in. He's in the study."

Trixie pushed open the door of the study and wandered off. Agatha went in. Arthur was sitting at his desk with George Selby.

Agatha was taken aback at the sight of George. She had forgotten how very handsome he was. "Come in. Sit down," said Arthur. "Arnold has just left. We have more or less finished working out where the money goes. Do you have the safe deposit key? We are going to transfer the money into an account and then, when the chequebook is issued, we will start sending out cheques."

"The police have the key," said Agatha. "Someone tried to break into my cottage, so I thought the key was safer there. If I had thought of it at the time, it might have been more sensible to deposit it in an account right away."

"We all agreed to the safe deposit box," said Arthur. "At that time, it seemed more sensible than having chequebooks lying around before we had worked out who gets the money apart from what is needed for the repairs to the roof. So many people seem to just walk into the vicarage during the day. I am sure everyone in the village is honest, but, just in case, we let everyone know that the money was in the safe deposit box. I'll drive Arnold over to . . . Mircester, is it?"

"Yes."

"We'll pick up the key soon and arrange a time to go to the bank. Is this a social call?"

"I just wanted to make sure you were satisfied that Sybilla Triast-Perkins put LSD in the jam."

"Alas, yes. I am afraid the poor lady had been behaving oddly these past few months. So sad. But such a relief to have the whole matter solved. I sent you a cheque for your services."

"Thank you. I'm afraid I wasn't much help."

"My dear lady, it is because of you that we will be able to repair the church."

George's grass-green eyes fastened on Agatha's face. Could they really be that green? Or could he be wearing contact lenses?

"Mrs. Raisin . . ."

"Agatha, please."

"Agatha. Can it be that you have doubts about the police verdict?"

"Well, I can't help wondering how Sybilla got hold of something like LSD."

"Have the police confirmed it was LSD?"

"Wait a minute." Agatha took out her phone and called Jimmy Wilson on his mobile. "Jimmy, I forgot to ask you, was it LSD in the jam at Comfrey Magna?"

She listened carefully, thanked him and rang off. "Yes, she said. LSD it was. So how did she get her hands on it? If it was a young woman, I could imagine her getting it at a club, although even that's odd because it's all Ecstasy and heroin and cocaine these days, not to mention some lethal-type pot grown in greenhouses. She wasn't a chemist at some time in her life?"

"As far as we know, she never worked," said George. "But perhaps she had a wild youth and had some left over."

"But why did her suicide note refer to one death and not two?"

Said the vicar, "She could hardly have been in a normal state of mind when she wrote it. Her sister is at the manor at the moment. You could ask her. But really, Agatha, our little village has settled back into its usual tranquil ways. The funerals of Mrs Andrews and Mrs. Jessop were very moving and yet healing in their way. We were all united in our grief."

"I think I'll go to the manor," said Agatha. "The sister, Mrs. Unwin, might have something interesting to say."

"Perhaps now might not be a good time," said George. "The poor woman must still be grieving."

"Oh, right," said Agatha.

She left the vicarage and found Charles waiting by her car. "I thought I might find you here," he said. "What's all this about suicide at the manor?"

Agatha gave him all the details and her suspicions

that Sybilla's suicide note had been referring to the murder of Sarah Selby rather than the jam at the fête.

"I've been warned off at the vicarage against going to see her," she finished by saying.

Charles grinned. "And that's not going to stop you?"

"No."

"Right. Leave your car and we'll take mine."

The rain was coming down in torrents by the time they reached the manor. The door was standing open.

"Anybody home?" called Agatha. Rainwater was dripping through the roof into several buckets placed about the hall.

A plump, fussy woman appeared in the hall. "What do you want?"

"Mrs. Unwin?"

"Yes?"

"I am Agatha Raisin . . ."

"You're that wretched woman who started all this off by interfering in the village fête! Get out of here."

"And this," said Agatha loudly, "is Sir Charles Fraith."

Oh, the magic of a title, thought Agatha cynically, as Mrs. Unwin visibly thawed. "I suppose it will do no harm to speak to you for a little," she said. "Come into the drawing room. Would you like some tea or coffee, Sir Charles?"

"It's all right," said Charles. "You've obviously got a lot to do with all these leaks."

"That was so like my sister," complained Cassandra Unwin as she led the way into the sitting room. "Never had any repairs done."

"Will you sell this place?" asked Charles.

"I'll need to fix it up. Mind you, a builder would pay a lot for it. Knock down the house and put a housing estate on the land."

"Wasn't this your family home?" asked Agatha.

"We grew up here, but I don't have any happy memories. If Sybilla hadn't insisted on hanging on to the place, she might have made a better life for herself. But suicide! I can't take it in. She can't have been responsible for anything like putting LSD in the jam. Where would she get it?"

"Your sister only referred to one death in her note," said Agatha, "and yet there were two caused by the LSD."

"Well, I don't suppose she was sane when she wrote that."

"I believe she was very fond of a Mr. George Selby," said Agatha, cautiously feeling her way through what she saw as a minefield of difficult questions.

"She talked a lot about him. I think she even had a sort of schoolgirl crush on him. Why do you ask?"

Charles saw that Agatha was going to jump in with

both metaphorical hobnailed boots, and said hurriedly, "We wondered whether he had called on you. Perhaps he might have a better idea as to your sister's state of mind."

"Then why don't you ask him? Really! I have a lot to do and I cannot see the point of all these questions."

Charles thanked her and, taking a reluctant Agatha by the arm, propelled her outside. "It's no use," he said. "You're not going to get anywhere. You can't come right out and ask her if Sybilla murdered George's wife. She won't have a clue anyway."

"Let's go and see Maggie Tubby and Phyllis Tolling. They're the ones who put the idea in my head."

The rain was still pouring down and they stood under an umbrella on the porch of the cottage in the main street, which seemed to be rapidly turning into a river behind them.

Phyllis opened the door. "You again. I thought the case was closed."

"Not quite," said Agatha.

"Come in."

Maggie was reading a book in the front parlour. "Who's your friend?" she asked.

"This is Sir Charles Fraith, who is helping me in the investigation."

"A 'sir,'" mocked Maggie. "How too terribly Dorothy Sayers. What do you want now?"

"Why did you suggest that Sybilla killed Sarah Selby?"

"We're sure she did. She was so unbalanced when it came to George. Now it looks as if she went even battier and tried to poison the village."

"But in her suicide note, she said she was sorry about a death. A death. Not two."

"You don't think she would be in exactly a sane state of mind," said Phyllis. "What's the matter with you? Trying to drum up some business? I tell you, the sooner that accountant gets to the bank and you give him that safe deposit key and he starts sending some money to the Andrews and Jessop families, the better it will be."

"How do you know about the safe deposit key?" demanded Agatha.

"It's all over the village. Everyone's been trying to get their hands on some of the money. Some claim that the visitors trampled over their gardens and ruined them—that sort of thing."

"So the only reason you think Sybilla killed Sarah Selby was a hunch?"

"Of course it was a hunch, you thickheaded creature. If we'd had any proof, we'd have gone to the police."

"Come along," said Charles. "The two witches haven't got anything important to say."

Maggie's eyes gleamed with mischief. "You don't like us, do you?"

"Who would?" said Charles.

———

Two days later, as the monsoon-like rain still continued to pour down, Agatha phoned her office. "I'll be a bit late," she said to Mrs. Freedman. "I'm going into Evesham to get my hair done."

"You can't, in this rain. Evesham'll be drowned."

"That's down in the town. My hairdresser is in Bridge Street and it never gets flooded. I'll go in by the ring road."

"You'd better watch your village doesn't flood."

"Carsely *never* floods."

"It might this time."

Agatha noticed as she drove over the Simon de Montfort Bridge on the ring road that the river Avon had already flooded and was spreading rapidly out over the farmland on either side.

Although the traffic was moving easily on her side of the road, the other side seemed to be grid-locked.

She parked in the Aldi supermarket car park and walked through to Bridge Street. Outside Achille, the hairdresser's, she turned and looked down towards the bridge. Police barriers were up. She walked down and joined the crowed of sightseers on the bridge. Waterside on the other side of the bridge was flooded. A large mobile home came hurtling down the river and smashed into the bridge. Bits of it appeared on the other side as if it had been through a giant shredder.

Agatha debated whether to return home while there was still time, but without her hair done she felt insecure.

Jeanelle, her hairdresser, greeted her with surprise. "We've been phoning up clients telling them not to come," she said.

Agatha's mobile rang. It was Toni. "We're evacuating the office," she said. "The police have been round telling us the water's rising. The street below is flooded. We're on the first floor, so with luck the water won't come this high. But Phil's found a man with a tractor and we've all been loading up the files and computers. The car park's still dry, so once the tractor gets the stuff there, we can load it into our cars and take it to a storage unit we've rented on high ground."

"It's really bad, isn't it?" said Agatha.

"Nobody's seen anything like it."

"Phone you later," said Agatha.

But she insisted on getting her hair done.

As she joined the queue inching out of Evesham, she wished she had never come. She had complained about the rap music playing in the hairdressing salon. It had crashed around her ears sounding like "Ugh, hunna hunna mudda fudda bitch, ugh."

"Who likes that awful music?" she had asked Jeanelle. "Young people," said the hairdresser. "It's our music, if you know what I mean."

I feel on the outside looking in, mourned Agatha. I feel trapped in an age group that's out of touch with every other age group.

It took her three hours to reach the Carsely turn-off on the A44 by managing to plough through areas of flooding on the road.

When she got down to just before the centre of the village, she was met by a flood. Groaning, she parked the car, took off her shoes and began to wade through the swirling water. A dead cat floated past and a spasm of fear clutched her as she thought of her own cats.

The rain was still falling in torrents. She slipped and stumbled, several times nearly falling, until at last she reached dry ground on the other side. Agatha put on her shoes and hurried to Lilac Lane. Water was swirling down the lane. She rushed to her cottage. Charles had barricaded the front door with sandbags.

Agatha let herself in. He had left her a note on the kitchen table.

"Gone to check my own place. Keep dry! Love, Charles."

Agatha checked her cats were safely indoors before going upstairs to change into dry clothes.

"It can't get any worse," she muttered.

But it did. Gloucestershire and the counties round about went under water. Her cottage stayed dry, but she had to house three elderly couples from the village who complained constantly that all the food she seemed to have were microwave curries.

Just when Agatha felt like committing murder herself, the sun came out and the waters receded. With great relief she saw her unwanted house guests leave. But then she was drafted in by Mrs. Bloxby to help clean out flooded cottages and to make frequent trips to the supermarket in Stow to bring back supplies of bread and milk.

At last she was free to go to her office in Mircester. Her staff were all there, unloading computers and other office equipment.

Gradually everything got back to normal and Agatha was just considering one evening whether to pursue the Comfrey Magna poisoning when she received a visit from Bill Wong.

"Survived the floods, Bill?"

"Just about. Agatha, this isn't a social call."

"What's happened?"

"Someone masquerading as Arnold Birntweather, the accountant, and with all his identification called at the bank with the safe deposit key. He said the money needed to be counted again. He put it all in a large holdall and disappeared. In appearance, he seemed to be like the accountant, elderly and stooped."

"But did the police hand this impostor the key?"

"They seem to have handed it over to the genuine man just after the flooding was over. He was accompanied by the vicar. When the vicar did not hear from him, he called at his house. Mr. Birntwweather had been killed by a savage blow to the head."

"But they had seen Mr. Birntweather at the bank before."

"Mr. Birntweather was old, with a dowager's hump, thick glasses and dyed brown hair. The impostor looked exactly like that."

"But how did the impostor get the number of the safe deposit box?" asked Agatha.

"Arnold Birntweather had a card inside his wallet with the number of the box on it. It was conveniently marked, 'Safe deposit box number eleven.'"

"Snakes and bastards! When I went to see that precious pair, Tolling and Tubby, they told me that everyone in the village knew I had the safe deposit key, which probably explains the break-in at my cottage."

"Do be careful, Agatha. I'd better get back to work."

"Wait a bit. What about fingerprints?"

"Everyone knows about fingerprints these days."

"CCTV cameras at the bank?"

"There's a thought. You'd better come to headquarters with me and look at the film. See if you can penetrate that disguise somehow and recognize someone from that village."

At police headquarters, Agatha studied the security tape film. Bill waited impatiently.

"Well?" he demanded at last.

"It's odd," said Agatha. "But I really do think that's Arnold."

"Mr. Birntweather?"

"Yes. I don't think any impostor could be that good. Have you any footage of the street outside the bank?"

"I'll run it for you. Why?"

"Maybe someone was waiting for him—someone who had threatened him."

Bill slotted in another tape. Agatha saw Arnold climbing stiffly out of his old Morris Minor. "Look!" said Agatha.

"What?"

"Run that again. A car with tinted windows pulled in right behind him."

"This is a very long shot, Agatha. I'll check the number plate. Wait there."

Agatha continued to study the tapes.

Then the door opened and Bill, Wilkes and Collins came in. Bill said, "You're on to something. That car was stolen during the floods. It belongs to a respectable shopkeeper in Badsey."

"You can go now," said Collins.

"No 'thank you'?" demanded Agatha. "I thought you had gone to Scotland Yard. Did they send you back?"

"Just get out of here!" snapped Collins.

Bill escorted Agatha out. "I thought she'd gone," said Agatha.

"She did. But for some reason she came back and now we're stuck with her. Thanks, Agatha. You're a great help."

Before she drove off, Agatha phoned Charles on his mobile, but as usual, it was switched off. She couldn't text him a message because, even though she had a state-of-the-art mobile, not only did she not know how to text, she did not know how to take photographs or send e-mails. She phoned his home and for once she was in luck. Charles himself answered, rather than his man, Gustav, or his aunt. Agatha told him about the latest development.

"Where are you?" asked Charles.

"Just about to leave Mircester."

"I'll meet you at your cottage."

"Thank goodness it's dry at last," said Charles. "But it's cold. Mind if I light the fire?"

"Go ahead," said Agatha. "Doris has it all set and ready." Doris was Agatha's cleaner and about the only person in the village who called Agatha by her first name. "I'll fix the drinks."

When Charles was comfortably settled in an armchair, cradling a glass of whisky and watching the flames leap up the chimney, he asked, "Any ideas?"

"My money's on Trixie."

"Come on! The vicar's wife? Can you see her stealing a car and threatening poor Arnold?"

"I'm sure she deliberately tried to spoil the accounts."

"What's all this?"

Agatha lit a cigarette, scowled at it and put it out. Cigarettes in the morning tasted great, but later in the day, they'd lost their magic.

"I was with Roy, and Arnold and the vicar were sorting through the accounts at a table in the garden. Trixie arrived with a jug of lemonade and I swear she deliberately tipped it over the papers."

"And were they ruined?"

"Well, no. It was sunny. Remember sunshine? I suggested we pin them up to dry. Arnold told me they were okay. Now, if Trixie had been squirrelling some of the money away and doctoring the accounts, Arnold might have known about it, but straightened it out with the vicar, not wanting any scandal."

"I can't believe it. Look, there were a lot of unsavoury things going on during the floods. Cars left on dry ground were being stolen. The gossip about the safe deposit box could have spread out from beyond the village. Put on the news and see if there's anything."

"Let's see if they've done better than their coverage

of the floods. Hopeless. I had to turn on the radio to get any proper news. All there was on TV was some reporter's great face blocking off the screen talking to the man in the studio. And they were all in Tewksbury. It's the herd instinct. They've always had it. One reporter puts on his waders and stands in a flooded street in Tewksbury and the other reporters promptly head for Tewksbury to do the same, along with their cameramen. I'll try the BBC *24 Hour News*."

They waited patiently through the usual dismal round of international news until suddenly the announcer said, "The village of Comfrey Magna is in shock tonight." A brief summary of the disastrous fête and the theft of the money. "And now to our reporter, Alan Freeze, in Comfrey Magna, who interviewed the vicar, Mr. Arthur Chance, early this morning."

"I am here with the vicar, Mr. Arthur Chance, and Mrs. Chance. This must be a sad blow, Mr. Chance."

"It's a disaster," said Arthur Chance. Trixie stood beside him dressed in a long black gown with a low neck.

"I bet those breasts aren't real," muttered Agatha.

"I don't know what to do," Arthur went on, his voice trembling. "The church roof is leaking and there is no longer any money for the repairs." He burst into tears. Trixie pressed his head into her bosom and stared nobly into the camera.

"Mrs. Chance?" pursued the reporter.

"I must take my poor husband indoors," said Trixie.

"It is not only the church roof that the money was needed for but for the families of the two ladies who were killed during the fête." She tossed back her blonde hair but still managed to clutch her sobbing husband to her chest.

Her eyes filled with tears and she said with a little break in her voice, "Please help us."

Then she escorted her husband into the vicarage.

"And now to the Middle East," said the presenter.

"Switch it off," said Agatha. "What a performance!"

"It was pretty moving," said Charles.

"Oh, the vicar was genuine. But did you see how Trixie said 'Help us'? Not 'Help us find who did this terrible murder.' She's hoping for donations, and she'll get them."

Charles finished his drink. "You're too cynical. We'll pop over to Comfrey Magna in the morning." He stood up and stretched and yawned. "I'm off to bed." His eyes gleamed with mischief. "Coming with me?"

"My days of casual sex are over," said Agatha.

"Didn't know they'd ever started. Good night."

After he had gone, Agatha sat looking into the flames, her cats beside her on the sofa. She felt strangely empty and purposeless. For so long, her obsession for James, her ex-husband, had fuelled all her actions. She missed the roller coaster of emotions. She even missed the pain.

"At least I felt alive," she whispered to her uncaring cats.

The morning was cold, damp and misty as Agatha drove herself and Charles to Comfrey Magna. At one point she said to Charles, "I forgot to find out about Jimmy Wilson."

"What about him?" asked Charles.

"There's something unsavoury about him. I asked Patrick to find out why he took early retirement from the police force. He made a pass at Toni."

"Most men would. She gets prettier by the minute."

Agatha felt a stab of jealousy. She had promised Toni to hold a dinner party to further the girl's hopes with Harry Beam. Now she meanly decided not to do anything about it.

Agatha parked at the entrance to the village, just before the vicarage. A great lake of water lay across the road, fed by angry little streams rushing down from the hills.

"We'll need to paddle," said Charles. "I wouldn't risk driving through that if I were you."

"I'll see if I can see the ground underneath the water." Agatha got out of the car. She stared down at the water gloomily and then returned to Charles.

"We'll need to paddle."

"Right." Charles got out of the car, took off his socks and shoes and then his trousers. Agatha took off her shoes and hitched up her skirt.

Charles, holding his trousers, socks and shoes above his head, walked into the water. "Not too bad," he said. "It's only just up past my knees."

"There's the postal van outside the vicarage," said Agatha, fighting to keep her balance in the swirling water. "I've always come this way. The road in from the other end must be clear."

"He's unloading sacks of mail. The vicar's distress must have caused a lot of people to send money. Dry ground at last," said Charles. "We'll nip into the church and I'll put my trousers on. Don't want to shock the vicar's wife."

"You're kidding. Nothing could shock that one."

The church was cold and damp. Buckets full of rainwater lay on the floor and balanced on the altar and the pews.

Agatha shivered as she pulled on her shoes. "This is misery," she moaned.

"Never mind," said Charles. "Think of those poor bastards in Cheltenham and Tewksbury. No drinking water and up to their armpits in sewage."

"I can never feel grateful because of other people's misery," said Agatha piously. "Let's go. Hope the police aren't there or it'll be a wasted journey."

They were just about to emerge from the church when

Agatha saw Wilkes and Collins leaving the vicarage. She retreated, colliding into Charles. "The police are just leaving," she hissed. "Wait a minute. I wonder where their car is. I didn't see a police car." She peered round the church porch. A police car and driver drove in from the other end of the village. Wilkes and Collins got in and the car drove off.

"All clear," said Agatha. "Let's go."

It was George Selby who opened the door to them. Does he never work? wondered Agatha.

"Oh, it's you," said George. "This is hardly a good time. Everyone is grieving."

A merry peal of laughter sounded from the study.

"Doesn't sound like it," said Agatha. "Let us in."

George reluctantly stood aside. Agatha felt a little sexual tremor as she brushed past him and opened the door of the study. Arthur Chance and Trixie were slicing open envelopes, their faces radiant.

"Come in!" called Arthur when he saw them. "People are amazingly generous."

"I'm happy for you," said Agatha. "But I really want to find out who murdered poor Arnold Birntweather."

"The police are looking into that," said Trixie, slicing open another envelope and extracting a cheque. "Oh, George, darling, come and help me."

"I've got work to do. Mrs. Raisin . . ."

"Agatha, please."

"Agatha, may I have a word with you in private?"

Agatha followed him outside.

"They really are upset and grieving," said George, fastening those hypnotic eyes of his on Agatha's face.

"Doesn't sound like it. What can I do for you, George?"

"If you start asking them questions about Arnold's murder, it will really distress them."

"But the police have just left and they don't seem a bit distressed."

"Look, let's go for dinner tonight and I'll tell you anything you want to know."

Agatha brightened. "All right. Where and when?"

"The Cantonese restaurant in Mircester? Say at eight o' clock?"

"Right."

He suddenly smiled down at her and Agatha felt weak at the knees. Must get rid of Charles, she thought frantically.

Toni had invited a former school friend, Sharon, round to her flat that evening. She felt uneasily that she had been blackmailed into the invitation by Sharon complaining that Toni never saw any of her old friends.

Thanks to Agatha's generous salary, Toni had been at work on her flat since Harry had seen it. She had ripped up the carpet and polished the boards until they shone. They were now covered in brightly covered rugs she had bought at Mircester market. A new set of bookshelves ornamented one wall.

"This is ever so nice," said Sharon. She was a plump girl with masses of dyed red hair. Her crop top and low-slung jeans revealed a roll of fat and a fake ruby in her navel. "You've got a lot of books." There was one lying on the coffee table. Sharon picked it up. "*Swann's Way* by Marcel Proust. Didn't we get that at school?"

"No, none of us read much at school. We got the university notes on books and read them instead."

"So why are you reading a book by some Frenchie? Marcel. Sounds like a hairdresser."

Toni's desire to talk about Harry overcame her. He hadn't been able to come to Mircester because of the floods, but he had e-mailed her on her new computer and texted her regularly. In his messages, he suggested which books she should read and the type of music she should listen to.

"It's my new boyfriend," said Toni. "He's studying at Cambridge. He's awfully clever. I did ask him for suggestions as to what I should read and I've been out buying piles of books."

Sharon, whose idea of a good read was the sort of magazine which described the private lives of celebrities along with other important female essentials like the type of vibrator to use, said, "I dunno if I'd like a chap like that."

"Why?" demanded Toni, immediately on the defensive.

"Well, it's like Kylie, remember her?"

"What about her?"

"She's tied up with Wayne. Remember Wayne?"

Toni conjured up a memory of a gangling spotty youth who'd been in her class.

"What about him?"

"He and Kylie are an item. Got a flat out on the Evesham road. No sooner have they moved in together than he starts telling her what to wear. Dowdy clothes. He's even got her to wear a cardigan and flat heels."

"I don't see the connection," complained Toni.

"He's making her over, don't you see? And that's what your fellow's doing. Either the fellows like you for what you are or tell 'em to get stuffed."

"It's not the same. He knows I want to improve my mind."

Sharon tossed back her thick hair. "Listen, babes, there isn't a fellow out there who's interested in a girl's mind. If they start making you over, it's because they want to control you and keep you feeling inferior so you'll end up thinking no other boy will want you."

"Oh, let's talk about something else," said Toni. "How's your love life?"

Agatha told Charles that she had to go back to the office to catch up on work. "Don't you want to go home and get some dry shoes?" asked Charles.

"I've got a change of clothes in the office, Charles. Are you staying tonight? I have to warn you I might be late."

"Don't sound so frantic, Agatha. Has George asked you out?"

Mulish silence.

"Aha. Okay, I'll clear off. What's he after?"

"He's going to give me everything he can think of that might give me a clue as to who murdered Arnold."

"And you don't want me along because at one point in the dinner, he will reach across the table and take your hand and say he thought he could never find anyone to replace his wife, but now—"

"Oh, do shut up!"

Agatha really wanted to go home and spend a leisurely time getting ready for the evening, but Charles might hang around making sarcastic comments up until she left. The only reason she had said she was going to the office was to get rid of him.

She dropped him off at her cottage, turned the car around and sped back to Mircester.

Agatha was determined to buy something dazzling to wear. But the weather was a problem. It was actually cold. If the lowering sky sent down any more torrents, it might be better not to wear anything too filmy and seductive.

She settled on buying a black wool trouser suit, black court shoes with a modest heel, and a scarlet silk blouse.

With a flutter of anticipation she had not felt in ages, Agatha began to dream about the evening to come.

Chapter Seven

THE RESTAURANT was called the Moulmein Pagoda. Agatha wondered whether the owner was a Kipling fan. She remembered how she and her school friends had found an old wind-up gramophone in a skip. It had one record on the turntable, "The Road to Mandalay." They had wound it up and played the record. Agatha had thought it romantic, but as soon as the record had finished, her companions had gleefully set about stomping on the record and gramophone until nothing was left but little pieces. She remembered the line, "By the old Moulmein Pagoda/Looking lazy at the sea," because in later years, she had looked up the poem in the library and had memorized it. But the pagoda had been in Burma and the sailor had been looking to China across the bay.

George was late. She ordered herself a mineral water and lit up a cigarette. Soon the smoking ban would be in force. The police were setting up a hotline where you could report anyone smoking on a free phone line. Of course, if you wanted to report a real crime, it would cost you fifty pee a minute. The powers that be were also going to send out undercover agents to restaurants and pubs. Soon it will be the obesity police, thought Agatha, snatching cream cakes from the jaws of ladies in tea shops.

After half an hour, Agatha decided to leave. She was just getting to her feet when George hurried in.

"Sorry I'm a bit late," he said.

"Half an hour, to be exact," Agatha pointed out.

"Sorry, sorry. Busy, busy."

He called the waiter over and said, "We'll have the number-two menu please. Would you like some wine, Agatha?"

"Do you think I might be allowed to choose it?" asked Agatha sarcastically.

"Of course. They do a very nice house white here."

"Where is the wine list?"

"On the back of the menu."

"I always think white wine goes better with Chinese food," said George.

"I like red," said Agatha firmly. "I'll have a half bottle of Merlot. What do you want?"

"I'll have a small carafe of the house white."

He shouldn't have ordered the meal for me, thought Agatha angrily. Why do I always get to know cheapskates? Probably frightened I would start choosing from the à la carte.

Aloud, she said, "I was wondering if the owner was a fan of Kipling."

"Why?"

"The restaurant's called the Moulmein Pagoda. That's from 'The Road to Mandalay'."

"Don't know it."

"It goes like this . . ."

To George's horror, Agatha began to sing in a loud alto soprano. A group at the other end of the restaurant joined in. There was a round of applause when Agatha finished and she stood up and bowed.

"Oh, do sit down and stop making a spectacle of yourself," snapped George.

But Agatha didn't care what he thought. He had left her waiting for half an hour and then had chosen her dinner.

"Do not . . . *ever* . . . speak to me like that again," said Agatha in a level voice. "You are neither my husband nor my father. Would you like me to leave?"

"No. Look—let's start again. I'm still upset at Arnold's death. Have the police any idea who broke into your cottage? It must be the same person who killed Arnold and stole the money."

Agatha sighed. "If it were a television programme, some forensics scientist would hold up one bit of hair and say, 'Aha! This matches the DNA of Arthur Chance or whoever.' But the police are probably sitting on their hands because it's me and it's only a burglary where nothing was stolen. Have you any idea at all who could have killed Arnold? You said you'd fill me in."

Suddenly in Agatha's mind that last sentence seemed to have a sexual connotation. She flushed and studied her glass of Merlot.

"I know that Arthur phoned Arnold on the day he was murdered and said they should both go to the bank that afternoon. Then he got a phone call from a Mrs. Wilmington, who was once a parishioner, pleading for his spiritual help and saying that she was close to death. So Arthur phoned Arnold and put the appointment off until the following day, because Mrs. Wilmington had given him an address in Warwick.

"When he got to the address in Warwick, he found it was a betting shop and no one in the flats above had ever heard of Mrs.Wilmington. He returned to the vicarage and looked up her last address, which was in Ancombe. He phoned. Mrs. Wilmington answered the phone, claimed she was fit and well and had never phoned him."

"Didn't he immediately call the police?"

"No, he thought it was someone playing a tiresome joke."

"So there's now a woman in the case. Probably a woman working in partnership with some man." Agatha silently cursed the police. They had held back all this from her.

"Let's talk about something else. Ah, here's our food. Tell me how you came to start a detective agency?"

In between eating and drinking, Agatha gave him a highly embroidered version of the cases she had solved and how she had at last decided to turn professional.

Then she realized that George had ordered another bottle of wine for her. "I'll need to take a taxi," said Agatha. "Oh, well, tell me about yourself. I've done all the talking."

George began. He was an architect and had settled in the Cotswolds because there were so many demands for house extensions and garage conversions. He was kept very busy. Of course, in a couple of cases, his clients had declared bankruptcy and he had not received any money for months of work. "I hadn't realized until I moved to the Cotswolds that bankruptcy had become a sort of growth industry. I mean, I knew there were a lot around, but I thought it was from people who had used too many shop credit cards charging high interest."

"You must miss your wife very much," said Agatha, mellowed with wine.

He heaved a sigh. "Sarah was such a homebody. She made all the curtains herself when we moved in, and loose covers for the chairs. Her cooking was plain but delicious. She never had any ambition. When we were in financial difficulties, I suggested she might like to get a job to help out. But she cried and said our home was her job."

"What about Fred Corrie?" asked Agatha, thinking

that perhaps George was attracted to the useless clinging type.

"What about her?"

"Does she work?"

"She paints. Watercolours. Don't sell very well, but
she's got an income from a family trust. Did anyone ever
tell you that you are a very sexy woman"?

Agatha blinked. Then she said, "Maybe."

He laughed and called for the bill. "I'll take you home
in a taxi. We can pick up our cars tomorrow."

In the darkness of the taxi, he reached out and took
her hand. He said softly, "I think our evening is not over
yet."

Agatha took rapid inventory of her body. Legs—yes,
shaved. Armpits, ditto. Was she ready for this? *Yes,*
screamed her hormones.

As the cab drew up outside her cottage, she saw all
the lights were on inside. "That's odd," said Agatha. "I
think someone's in there."

George curtly told the taxi to wait. Agatha unlocked
the door and marched straight into the sitting room.
Charles was lying on the sofa, one leg in plaster propped
up on a cushion.

"What happened to you?" raged Agatha.

"I fell down your stairs and broke my leg," said
Charles plaintively. "I called the ambulance and got
fixed up."

"Why didn't you go home?"

"Aunt's away and Gustav is on a break, so I decided you'd be the best person to look after me, light of my life."

"I'd better go," said George.

Agatha saw him to the door. "Charles is just a friend," she said.

"Oh, really? 'Night."

After he had gone, Agatha marched back inside. Charles was sitting upright on the sofa. Beside him on the floor was the discarded plaster cast, looking like a white umbrella stand.

"What in hell's name were you playing at?" raged Agatha.

"Calm down. No, don't shout. Listen. George Selby is a suspect, or had you forgotten? Ever since you've got over James, you've been desperate for a replacement. Think about it. Were you really going to fall into bed with a man who might have organized the death of his wife? A man who may even have killed poor Arnold?"

Agatha sat down beside him on the sofa. "How did you know I might come back with him?" she asked sulkily.

"Because it's just the sort of dangerous thing you've done in the past."

"Where did you get the cast?"

"I got it from Mrs. Bloxby's theatrical costume basket."

"You *told* Mrs. Bloxby."

"No, I said I needed something to make me look as if I had been injured because I wanted to get out of doing something. That excellent lady did not ask any questions. The amateur dramatic society put on a show of *Carry On Doctor* about five years ago. Want a drink?"

"I've had enough. Do you really think George is involved in any of this?"

"Not sure. Does he spend a lot of time at the vicarage?"

"He does seem to be there a lot."

"Why? Does he strike you as having the character of a do-gooder?"

"He could be. He organized all those marquees for the fête."

"I can't see a successful architect having much time for anything else other than work. Where's his office?"

"I don't know."

"It might be worthwhile finding out and sending someone from your office he doesn't know to suss out the place."

"I'll think about it. I'm going to bed."

Agatha hesitated in the doorway. "Thanks," she said gruffly. "I could have made an awful fool of myself."

"Oh, dear Agatha," said Charles, "don't start growing up. It alarms me. You should be throwing things at my head."

Before Agatha left for the office the next morning, Patrick phoned her. "I thought I'd better tell you this before you come in," he said. "You asked me to find out about Jimmy Wilson. Yes, he did have bowel cancer, but that wasn't the reason he retired. He was cured and back at work. He was sent out to cover a case. A woman had been raped in her home. Jimmy was accompanied by another detective, Miriam Wells. Miriam escorted the woman down to the rape unit while the forensic team went over her flat. Jimmy stayed behind. The rapist was caught through his DNA, which was on file, but before his arrest, the woman claimed that five thousand pounds she kept in a drawer in her bedroom had been taken. She was told the rapist must have taken it. She said no. While she was waiting for the police, she had looked into the drawer and had seen the money was still there.

"After a long investigation, it was suggested to Jimmy that he should take early retirement."

"Why did they think it was him? It could have been one of the forensic team or that Miriam detective."

"The fact is that there had been a couple of cases Jimmy had been on before in which money had gone missing. In each case, Jimmy was suspected, but nothing was proved."

"Tell Jimmy to follow up on that factory case, the one with the missing goods, and the rest of you come over here."

Agatha knew Charles was asleep upstairs in the spare bedroom. She decided to let him sleep. She still felt ashamed of the fact that she had been so ready to leap into bed with George and didn't want to be reminded of the fact first thing in the morning.

She hurried along to the village shop and bought a large bag of croissants. Back home, she put on a pot of coffee and then set the kitchen table with strawberry jam, butter and sugar, plates and knives, cream and milk.

Agatha opened the garden door and let her cats out and then lit a cigarette. Her mind seemed to be leaping all over the place.

When her staff, minus Jimmy, arrived, she waited until they were all seated around the table with plates of croissant and mugs of coffee before she began.

"I have learned something upsetting about Jimmy. Tell them, Patrick."

They all listened carefully. When Patrick had finished, Toni exclaimed, "I knew there was something awful about him."

"The fact is this," said Agatha. "I'm worried now that Jimmy might have been the one who stole the church money and murdered poor old Arnold. If that turns out to be the case, it's going to look bad for the agency. Who's going to trust us in the future?"

"I can't see Jimmy going as far as murder," said Patrick.

"I'd like a watch kept on his house," said Agatha. "The trouble is, he knows all of us."

Charles ambled in wearing his dressing gown.

"What sort of place does he live in?" asked Toni. "Is it a house or a flat? Is it on a busy road?"

"Wait a minute," said Agatha. "His address is on my computer. I'll check."

She came back after a few minutes. "He lives in Evesham. Port Street."

"Wasn't that flooded out?" said Phil.

"He didn't mention it or take time off, so it must be the top end. He probably lives over a shop."

"I could do it," said Toni.

"He knows you."

"He only knows me like this. Believe me, he won't recognize me."

"I don't want you running into any danger," said Agatha.

"I could park my car outside," said Phil. "With glasses and a tweed cap pulled down, he wouldn't know me. He's always sneering at me and calling me 'grandad.' Patrick can scrunch down in the back seat. Then, when Jimmy goes out, Patrick can break into his flat. It's no use protesting, Patrick. I know you've got a set of skeleton keys."

"Going to be right difficult," said Patrick. "The long-light nights are here. Say he lives up at the top end of

Port Street, well, it's pretty deserted at night. Then, if it's just the one flat above a shop, I'll look conspicuous standing there fiddling with the lock."

"Can't you send him away somewhere?" suggested Charles.

"You might have something there. He's also got the Tropper case. Mrs. Tropper suggests her husband might be taking his totty to a hotel in Brighton. That's it. I'll send him off tomorrow."

"What if I take Mrs. Freedman with me for the break-in?" said Patrick. "Jimmy's some relative of hers."

"She'd be too shocked and she might say something to him."

"Right. We'll just send him on his way tomorrow and then decide what to do about it."

Agatha could not believe her luck the next morning when she found Jimmy, stretched out on the sofa, fast asleep. The office was full of stale beer fumes. His jacket was hanging over the back of a chair. She felt in the pockets and extracted his keys. Quietly she let herself out and rushed to the nearest key cutters. She looked at her watch. Ten to nine. The shop door was closed. She impatiently rattled the handle. The blind on the door was raised and the shopkeeper mouthed, "Closed," and pointed to his watch.

Agatha opened her handbag and took a twenty-pound note out of her wallet and waved it. The door opened. "I need an extra set of house keys," said Agatha. "Twenty pounds over the price if you do it now."

Soon she had the keys copied and hurried back to the office. Jimmy was sitting up, staring blearily around.

Agatha walked towards her desk and knocked his jacket to the floor as she did so. She slipped Jimmy's keys on top of the jacket and then rounded on him.

"What where you doing sleeping in the office?"

"I had a bit of a bevvy last night," said Jimmy. "Too many coppers around, so I decided to sleep it off here."

"You'd better go home and get a bath and then take yourself off to Brighton. It's the Tropper case. Mrs. Tropper thinks he's taking his bit of stuff to Brighton. He told her he was there on a sales conference. Check and see."

Jimmy stood up. "I'll get off. I'll need an advance for expenses."

Agatha unlocked the office safe and took out a wad of notes. "I want you to account for every penny of that."

"Sure. See you. Bye."

The rest of Agatha's staff were all out on jobs. She telephoned each of them to say she had the keys and they all said they would come back in for a council of war. She suggested they meet at the Sorrento Café in

Mircester so that Mrs. Freedman wouldn't know what they were up to. She phoned Charles as well, but he said he had to go home to deal with things.

Agatha could only hope and pray that Jimmy would not turn out to be the culprit. Such a scandal would hit the agency hard.

When they were all seated in the café, Agatha said, "Toni and I had better go. We'd be less conspicuous."

"Are you sure?" asked Phil. "I could come along as bodyguard."

Agatha looked affectionately at Phil's elderly face and white hair and said, "We'll be all right. Jimmy's not going to hurry back from an expenses-paid trip to Brighton."

Jimmy's flat turned out to be at the top end of Port Street near the garage above a small grocery store.

They were not wearing any disguises. Agatha had said that she had a good excuse. She could say she had forgotten she had sent Jimmy to Brighton and was checking up on him.

There were two keys on the ring. Agatha correctly guessed that the bigger of the two opened the street door.

Inside, worn stone steps led up to the floor above. "Good," Agatha whispered. "Only one door. No neighbours."

She unlocked the door and they both went in. "What a tip!" exclaimed Agatha. Empty beer cans lay about the floor. Empty pizza boxes were piled up on the coffee table. "Oh, well, hold your nose and let's get started. Try to put everything back the way it was. Here's a pair of gloves."

It was only a tiny flat, consisting of one living room, one bedroom and a minuscule kitchen. The bathroom contained a shower so small, Agatha wondered how Jimmy managed to get his bulk into it. They worked steadily, searching cupboards and under the bed, in the bathroom cistern and even making a slit in the side of the mattress in case Jimmy had stuffed the money in there.

Agatha began to feel quite cheerful. She really didn't want Jimmy to be the culprit. "Give up!" she called to Toni, who was still searching the bedroom. "I'm beat."

She carefully removed two newspapers from a plump armchair and collapsed into it with a sigh of relief. Then she stiffened and slowly stood up. "Toni, come here!"

"Found anything?" asked Toni, coming through from the bedroom.

"The big seat cushion on that armchair feels as if it's stuffed with something."

"Let's have a look." Toni picked up the huge seat cushion. "It's been clumsily stitched up at the back," she said. "I've got a pair of nail scissors in my handbag."

"If there's nothing sinister in there, we're going to

have to try to stitch it up again so that it looks the same," said Agatha.

Toni took the scissors out of her handbag and cut the threads. "There's something here," she said. She grabbed hold of the end of something and pulled. Agatha stared. She found herself looking at a familiar bank bag.

"We can just take it," said Toni eagerly, "and give it back to the church. Fire Jimmy and there'll be no scandal."

"Can't," said Agatha. "You forget Arnold was murdered. I'll call the police. I'll say I had more instructions for Jimmy. He didn't answer his phone. We came up here and found the door open. No Jimmy. I sat in that armchair and I thought, there's something in this cushion, and blah, blah, blah."

"Sounds thin."

"Got any better ideas?" Agatha took out her phone and called police headquarters in Mircester.

She managed to get hold of Bill Wong and spoke rapidly. When she had finished, Toni said nervously, "Do you think they'll search us?"

"Probably not. Why?"

"You've got the keys and we've both got latex gloves."

"I'll attach the keys to my own key ring and we're supposed to carry latex gloves. We're detectives."

"This is Evesham. Won't it be Worcester police?"

"It's Gloucester's case. I think they'll come straight

here and let Worcester know afterwards. I feel a bit shaky now. Poor Mrs. Freedman. She's going to be shattered by this bit of news."

"I've thought of something!" exclaimed Toni.

"What?"

"They'll automatically search the flat for fingerprints."

"We were wearing gloves."

"Don't you see? That's it. Why were you wearing gloves?"

"Let me think. I know. We found the money right off because I sat down for a rest. We thought we may as well look round while we were waiting."

"Won't work. They'll know that we'll know a crime scene shouldn't be touched."

"We'll tell them we wanted to find out where Jimmy was staying in Brighton, if he had left a note somewhere."

"And they'll say, 'Why didn't you phone him?'"

"Couldn't get an answer."

"What if they check your phone records?"

"Snakes and bastards," howled Agatha. "I'm not the villain here."

"Mrs. Raisin?" Agatha swung round. Wilkes and Collins were standing in the doorway. Just behind them stood Bill Wong.

"Where is the money?" asked Wilkes.

Agatha pointed to the armchair cushion. "It's in there."

"How did you find it? This is Jimmy Wilson's flat, isn't it? And he works for you."

Agatha told her tale of wanting to get in touch with Jimmy, who was in Brighton. She had sat down in the armchair and had felt all the paper inside it and decided to have a look. "So you don't know where he's staying?"

"I couldn't get him on the phone," said Agatha. "Knowing Jimmy, if he thinks he's richer than he was, he'll probably be staying somewhere grand."

Wilkes spoke rapidly into his phone, ordering someone at headquarters to contact the Brighton police and arrest Jimmy Wilson.

"Why did you employ such a person?"

"He's an ex-detective. He was one of your lot."

"I want you and Miss Gilmour to go directly to police headquarters to be interviewed. Detective Sergeant Wong will go with you."

At police headquarters, Agatha and Toni were split up. Agatha was interviewed by the terrible Collins and another detective called Finch.

The questioning was rapid-fire and bullying. Collins stopped just short of implying that Agatha had been in on the theft of the money and the murder of Arnold.

Grimly, Agatha stuck to her story, reminding Collins time after time that because Jimmy was a retired detective, she had no reason to suspect him.

At last, she was free to go but was warned that she

had to be ready for further questioning. She found Toni waiting for her.

"Let's go for a drink," said Agatha. "I wonder if they've caught Jimmy."

Jimmy strolled into the foyer of the Grand Hotel in Brighton. "One of your best rooms," he said to the clerk.

"Name, please, sir?"

"Wilson. James Wilson."

The clerk looked across the foyer and gave a little nod. Sweat began to run down Jimmy's fat face. He was suddenly frightened to turn around.

"Got that room?" he asked in a quavering voice.

A heavy hand landed on his shoulder. A deep voice said, "James Wilson, we are arresting you for the murder of Arnold Birntweather and the theft of funds belonging to the church of—"

He broke off because Jimmy, who had slowly turned round, was scrabbling at his shirt collar. "Air. Need air," he gabbled. Then one side of his face slipped and he fell to the ground, unconscious.

Jimmy died of a massive stroke on the road to hospital. In the following two weeks, Agatha coped with the guilt of Mrs. Freedman and all her fears that her business would slump. The murder of Arnold had been solved as far as the police were concerned, although they had been unable to track down Jimmy's female accomplice. Comfrey Magna was almost forgotten as Agatha's staff rushed to wrap up as many of their other outstanding cases as they could to prove their worth. They had even been working through the weekends.

Agatha at last called a halt. She announced they would all take the next weekend off. Toni received an excited phone call from Harry. He wanted to take her to a production of Prokofiev's *Lady Macbeth of Minsk*. A touring Russian company would be performing at the weekend in Mircester. Toni said she would like to go.

In anticipation of Harry's visit, she cleared all the women's magazines she liked to read out of her flat. She felt sure he would not approve.

Harry then texted her and said he had good seats for the matinee on Saturday afternoon. Toni felt relieved. She had been wondering what to wear. A Saturday-afternoon performance didn't seem to call for anything too grand. Besides, Harry had said he would have to leave for Cambridge after the show.

The weather was unusually chilly for summer, so she bought herself a smart dark-blue trouser suit at an up-market thrift shop. She wore a low top under it and three strings of fake pearls bought at the market. She tried out the outfit for her friend, Sharon.

"You look like a businesswoman," commented Sharon. "You don't look like someone going out on a hot date."

"I don't think opera is a hot date," said Toni. "He's trying to widen my experience."

"What about sex?"

"Haven't got round to that yet."

"Why?" demanded Sharon. "My latest squeeze can't keep his paws off me."

Toni frowned. "Maybe they do things differently in Cambridge."

Earlier that day, Harry had given his Cambridge girlfriend, Olivia, a hearty kiss before getting on his motorbike. Olivia was plump and pretty. Harry considered their current affair to be warm and uncomplicated. Before he drove off, Olivia said, "Remember *Pygmalion*."

"I'm just helping the girl," said Harry. "I'd make a good teacher."

When he reached Mircester, he parked his bike near the theatre and stripped off his protective leathers and helmet. He was wearing jeans and an open-necked checked shirt. He pulled a suede jacket out of his satchel and put it on. As he strolled towards the theatre, he ran into a group of his old school friends, who were just coming out of the pub. "We're going for a curry," said a tall gangly youth called Bertie Bryt-Anderson. "Coming?"

"No, I'm going to the opera. I'm waiting for a friend."

"Female friend?"

"Just a friend. Oh, that's her. Just about to cross the road."

Toni was waiting for the traffic light to change. Sunlight glinted on her fair hair.

"If that's just a friend, what about an introduction?" said Bertie. "What a looker!"

"I'd better go," said Harry.

Followed by cheers and wolf whistles, he hurried to meet Toni.

"What's that about?" asked Toni, looking towards the group of young men.

"Idiots! Never mind them."

Toni felt a flutter of anticipation as they took their seats in the stalls. This would be her first opera. The conductor arrived, the audience applauded and he raised his baton. After a few minutes, Toni whispered, "Is this it? Has it started?"

"It's the overture," hissed Harry.

Toni blushed miserably. The curtain rose on a large cage which dominated the stage. Toni tried to enjoy it, but it all seemed brutal and violent. The female worker the other workers tried to rape on the stage was actually stripped naked. She gave a sigh of relief when the interval arrived. "Do you know Stalin walked out when he first saw this opera?" said Harry eagerly as he ushered her to the bar.

"Really?" Toni miserably felt she might have done the same thing if she had been on her own.

Harry got himself a beer and Toni a glass of orange juice. He was just about to explain more about the opera to her when he found himself accosted by his former English teacher, Mark Sutherland.

"How's Cambridge?" asked Mark, his eyes fastened on Toni.

Mark was a tall, rangy man in his forties with a prominent nose and bright blue eyes.

"Going all right. Oh, Toni, this is my former English teacher, Mr. Sutherland. Mr. Sutherland, Miss Toni Gilmour."

"Call me Mark. We're not in school now." Mark had taken Toni's hand and was holding on to it. "Where did you find this beautiful lady?"

"Toni works for the detective agency that I used to work for."

"Indeed! How fascinating. I've always wanted to write a detective story. Perhaps, Toni, we could meet for a drink one evening and you can tell me about your work."

"Mark?"

He swung round impatiently and then his face fell. "May I introduce my wife, Pamela? I thought you didn't want to come to the bar, dear." Pamela was small and thin and dressed in a floaty Indian gown which sparkled with little bits of mirror. She had a thin, avid face and glittering black eyes, which she fastened on Toni.

"Well, here I am, *dear*. You introduced me but not them."

"Oh, sorry." As Mark had finished the introductions, the bell went, calling them back to their seats.

Toni sat down again. She felt terribly out of place. She did not understand the music and put it down to her lack of proper education in the arts.

Because of the time factor, there was only to be one interval, so she decided to sit back and think of other things until it was all over.

Harry glanced from time to time at her serene face. Her eyelids were lowered and he noticed how very long her eyelashes were.

When they at last emerged from the theatre and stood blinking in the sunlight, Toni turned round and, to Harry's surprise, shook him firmly by the hand. "Thank you very much for a most interesting experience. Gotta run."

And run she did, her slim figure weaving in and out of the pedestrians. Well, thought Harry, I did tell her I had to go straight back to Cambridge after the show. He had known she was pretty, but he had been so busy playing Pygmalion, "moulding her mind," as he described it to himself, that he had never rightly taken in that Toni could be someone that men of all ages might desire.

He also knew he should never have tried to show off by taking her to a Russian opera that quite a number of people might find difficult to listen to when they heard it for the first time.

And she had so firmly shaken his hand! Just as if he were some elderly uncle! Nobody shook hands much these days.

He drove off and Mircester receded behind him. By the time he reached the flat fields of Cambridgeshire, he felt himself somehow growing smaller in stature.

Toni wondered whether to go round to one of the discos that evening to dance the memory of that opera out of her head. But instead, she got into her car and headed for Carsely.

Agatha was rummaging in her deep freeze to see if she could unearth something for dinner. Most of the packets were frosted over and she scraped busily at some of them, trying to make out what they were. The doorbell rang. Agatha brightened. She belonged to that generation of women who still considered it a sign of failure to be alone on a Saturday night.

"Oh, it's you, Toni," she said on opening the door. "Come in. What's up?"

"Something's bothering me."

"Well, come in. Have you eaten?"

"Not yet."

"Maybe we'll go to the pub. I keep throwing stuff into the freezer and then I can never figure out what the stuff is. Yes, let's go to the pub and get a plateful of comforting cholesterol and you can tell me about it."

"Oh, they've got salads now," said Agatha, when they were seated in the pub. "Maybe . . . maybe not. Comfort food is what we need. What about steak and kidney pie and new potatoes?"

"Sounds good," said Toni.

"That's a very smart suit," commented Agatha, "but not like the things you usually wear. Sort of thing one wears for a job interview." Agatha's small eyes bored into Toni's face. "Not looking for another job, are you?"

"It's not that. Harry took me to the opera."

"This I must hear. Wait until I order the food at the bar." When Agatha came back after placing the order, she said, "So what happened? I didn't know you were seeing Harry."

"I wasn't, really. Not until today, that is. He had been texting me, telling me what music to listen to and what books to read."

"Why?"

"He was trying to improve my mind."

"Cheeky thing to do."

Toni sighed. "I thought my mind needed improving. I'm tired of this limbo feeling. You know, not really belonging anywhere."

"So what was the opera? I saw *Carmen* once. Great fun."

"It was by Prokofiev—*Lady Macbeth of Minsk*. I made an awful fool of myself. I didn't know what was happening at the beginning, the music sounded so weird, so I said, 'Is this it?' and it turned out to be the overture."

"Maybe we should ask Mrs. Bloxby," said Agatha. "I'm hardly the person to ask. Most of my life has been work, work, work. I can't understand Harry. Did he try to make love to you?"

"Never."

"I thought I knew that young man inside out, but when it comes to romance, I'm the world's greatest loser," said Agatha. "We'll have our food and then take a walk along to the vicarage. I've been thinking and thinking about that Comfrey Magna business. The police have more or less given up because they've come to the conclusion that it was a prank that went wrong. Somehow, I don't like to leave it."

"We could go there tomorrow," suggested Toni. "Now things have quieted down, people might be readier to talk. How's Charles?"

"Okay, I think. He is infuriating. I would have expected him to turn up when he heard all that scandal about Jimmy Wilson. Maybe he's on holiday. No, come to think of it, he's just behaving like his usual selfish self."

After they had eaten steak and kidney pie, followed by apple pie and custard, Agatha ordered two coffees, took out a packet of cigarettes and lit one up. John Fletcher, the barman, came hurrying over. "Put that damn thing out, Agatha. The smoking ban's started and you'll get me fined."

"Stalinist bureaucrats," grumbled Agatha. She saw for the first time that there was no ashtray on the table and handed the cigarette to John, who hurried off with it, holding it at arm's length as if it were a small stick of dynamite.

As they approached the vicarage, Agatha felt guiltily that they should have phoned first. Quite a number of people in the village took their troubles to Mrs. Bloxby, just as if the vicar's wife should be always there as a sort of personal therapist.

"We should have phoned," said Agatha. "I always make the mistake of just dropping in."

"Phone now," said Toni.

"We're practically on the doorstep."

"Phone anyway."

Agatha fished her mobile out of her bag. She had never learned how to store important numbers and so, instead of pressing a convenient button, she dialled the whole number.

"It's Mrs. Raisin here," said Agatha. "I'm with Miss Gilmour. We would like your advice."

Toni waited. Then she heard Agatha say, "We're actually practically on your doorstep . . . You're sure? Great."

The door opened as they approached. This must be what the fortunate feel like, coming home, thought Toni suddenly, looking at the slim figure of the vicar's wife with her gentle smile.

"It's quite a nice evening," said Mrs. Bloxby. "I'm sure you would rather sit in the garden and have a cigarette, Mrs. Raisin."

"Great. Just so long as one of the army of British snoops doesn't leap out from behind a gravestone in the churchyard."

"You're all right outside." Mrs. Bloxby led the way. "Would you like something to drink? Coffee?"

Toni shook her heard and Agatha said, "No, we're fine."

When they were seated under a pale green evening sky, Mrs. Bloxby asked, "Do you want my advice about anything to do with Comfrey Magna?"

"No, it's not that. But what about Comfrey Magna?"

"I just wondered how that case was going."

"Not anywhere at the moment," sighed Agatha. "The fact is, with all the scandal about Jimmy, we've all been working like beavers to clear up as many of the cases on our books as possible. I thought the shame of having someone like Jimmy as a detective would have ruined the agency, but it doesn't seem to have."

"So what do you want advice on?"

"It's Toni's problem. Tell her, Toni."

Toni gave her a full account, ending up with describing her experiences at the opera, meeting Harry's friends before it and his English teacher during the interval. "His English teacher even asked me out," she said, 'but then his wife joined us and she didn't look very happy. Harry had told me he had to go straight back to Cambridge after the show, so I shook hands with him and ran off."

"So I gather there was nothing romantic in your friendship," said Mrs. Bloxby.

"Nothing at all. He didn't seem interested in that side of things. Mind you, this was the first date I ever had with him apart from that trip to Comfrey Magna. But I guess it wasn't a real date."

"I am no music expert," said Mrs. Bloxby, "but I should think that particular work would be quite difficult for someone to enjoy who had not heard a great deal of Prokofiev's other music. I think Harry got carried away with the idea of being a sort of tutor. I am sure his friends found you very attractive, not to mention that English teacher. He will now see you in a new light. If he falls in love with you, would that trouble you?"

Toni bent her fair head. I wonder if I once had that bloom, that innocence, thought Agatha sadly.

Toni at last gave a reluctant laugh. "My friend, Sharon, said he was trying to make me over. She warned me against him. He made me feel silly and stupid and I don't think I'll ever forget that."

"Someone will come along for you when you least expect it," said Mrs. Bloxby. "But remember—you are now eighteen, are you not? Yes. Remember that the person you love at eighteen will probably not be the person you would love when you are, say, twenty-five. Mrs. Raisin knows you are a very clever girl. Reading good books and listening to classical music is a grand thing, but in your own time and at your own pace. There is one odd thing. The university term at Cambridge finished for the summer on June fifteenth. What is Harry still doing there?"

"I don't know."

"He has parents in Mircester, does he not?"

"Yes," said Agatha. "Since he doesn't want sex with Toni and he's still in Cambridge, he's probably shacked up with some bit of tottie."

Mrs. Bloxby looked quickly at Toni's downcast face. "You weren't in love with him, were you?" she asked.

Toni shook her head. "'I was flattered, that's all."

"University students are ten a penny," said Agatha bracingly, "but good detectives like you are very rare. I know. Work might take your mind off it. Let's go to

Comfrey Magna tomorrow and see if we can dig anything up."

I wonder what it is that *Mrs. Raisin* wants to take her own mind off, thought Mrs. Bloxby, but she did not say anything.

Chapter Eight

THE FACT WAS THAT Agatha had forgotten about George turning up half an hour late at the restaurant and that he had ordered her meal. What might have been a squalid night of sex that she would bitterly regret, her romantic mind turned into a dream opportunity that had been missed.

As she parked the car in Comfrey Magna the next morning, she said, "I would like to meet Fred Corrie again. See what you think of her. She's probably in church. We'll wait for her."

"Is that a good idea?" asked Toni. "She might come out with a bunch of people. Did she strike you as the sort of female to go to church?"

"Well, she was running that tombola stand, so probably. I know, we'll drive along to her cottage and wait."

The day was unusually cold. There were large heavy grey rain clouds on the horizon. "What a lousy summer it's turned out to be," mourned Agatha.

"It really is an odd village," said Toni. "So quiet."

"They're all probably in church."

"That's one of the things that's odd. It seems to me as if only a few old people go to church these days."

"There seem to be a lot of old people here." Agatha peered in the rear-view mirror. "Oh, God's waiting room full of villagers is just coming out."

"Do you see Fred?"

"Not yet. George is there." Agatha's heart gave a lurch. She had a sudden impulse to reverse right back up the village street to the church, but she controlled it.

"I think Fred is at home," said Toni. "I saw one of the curtains twitch. We'd better go and knock. She'll be wondering what on earth we're doing sitting here."

Agatha experienced a certain reluctance as she got out of the car. She knew Fred's fey appearance was going to make her feel lumbering and ungainly. If the chemists could ever come up with a bottle of something labelled "Self-Respect" that actually worked, they could make millions, she thought.

The door opened just as they arrived on the step. Fred, as dainty as ever, was wearing an emerald-green smock over white linen shorts, and her feet were bare. Her toenails were painted emerald green.

"Really sorry to trouble you again," began Agatha, "but I wanted to ask you some more questions."

"Such as? Oh, you'd better come in."

Although the windows were open, Toni smelled the faint scent of pot.

"Now what?" asked Fred. Agatha sank down onto a very low sofa and immediately regretted it. She twisted her legs sideways so as not to expose her knickers.

"I keep harking back in my mind to the morning of the fête," said Agatha. "You were out very early."

"I told you that," said Fred in a bored voice.

"Can you remember anything that might help? A sound?"

"Like what?"

"A car moving off, footsteps, someone scrabbling to unfasten the tent flap?"

"Just the usual dawn chorus."

"Have you lived in the village for long?" asked Toni.

"For five years."

"I wondered if you heard any gossip," pursued Toni. "Anything about anyone that might lead you to suspect them of being capable of putting LSD in the jam."

"I am used to country life," said Fred. "This is a tightly knit community. Most people are churchgoers. All very respectable."

"And yet," said Agatha, "there is a rumour that Mr. George Selby's wife was murdered by Miss Triast-Perkins."

"Rubbish! Utter rot! And why are you still poking about? Sybilla committed suicide and confessed."

"But in her suicide note she referred to one murder, only one."

"The woman was as nutty as a fruitcake. Are you

short of work or something, considering one of your own detectives took the church money and killed Arnold? Just go away and stop wasting my time."

She watched with cold eyes as Toni helped Agatha out of the depths of the sofa.

After Agatha had parked the car beside the churchyard wall, Agatha asked Toni, "What did you make of her?"

"She smokes pot."

"You sure?"

"Yes, she had opened the windows, but I could smell it."

"And to think she got so upset when I wanted to light up a cigarette! I tell you, it's positively PC these days to smoke pot but not nicotine."

"Not any longer," said Toni. "They say the new stuff on the market is so strong it causes things like schizophrenia."

"If she's into pot, she could be into something stronger, like acid."

"A lot of people smoke pot. It's easily come by," said Toni.

"I'd send you round the clubs trying to find LSD, but I don't want you to get into trouble again."

"It wouldn't work," said Toni. "Ever since I was on television on that last case, everyone will know I'm a detective and back off. I can ask my friend, Sharon. I wonder what the life of LSD is. Whether it has a sell-by date?"

"Why?"

"Because it might be an idea to find out if any of the suspects has had a wild youth."

Agatha frowned in thought. "We've got to start somewhere. I know, let's go to the vicarage and ask if they've got a collection of photographs of previous fêtes. See if anyone looks odd. Maybe they've got some old photographs."

"You mean like, say, Mrs. Glarely dressed as a hippy?"

"Something like that. We've really got nothing else to go on."

The vicar himself opened the door to them. "Can I help you?" His voice was unwelcoming. "The case is closed and the money has been returned—money taken by one of your detectives who, no doubt, murdered Arnold."

"True. But we recovered that money for you," said Agatha briskly. "We are still trying to find out who killed Mrs. Jessop and Mrs. Andrews."

"The police say it was probably a youthful prank gone wrong."

"I'd like to be sure."

"I do not see how I can be of any help to you."

"We wondered," said Toni, "if you had old photographs of the previous fêtes, going back a bit. We might see someone there who shouldn't be. I mean, all the previous ones must have been very small affairs."

The vicar hesitated. Then he said reluctantly, "I suppose there is no harm in your looking. You must come and wait. I have boxes and boxes of them in the attic."

"I'm sure you're awfully busy," said Toni eagerly. "Just lead us up to the attic and we'll do the searching ourselves."

The vicar looked relieved. When they had reached the first landing, Trixie appeared at the foot of the stairs and called out, "Where are you taking them?"

"Just to the attic. They want to look at our old photographs."

"Whatever for?"

"I'll tell you when I come down."

As in all old Cotswold buildings, the stairs grew steeper as they climbed higher. Agatha's bad hip gave a sinister twinge, reminding her that the hip injection she had paid for had been responsible for the recent absence of pain, and not, as she had desperately hoped, to the fact that she had not been suffering from arthritis at all.

Arthur Chance threw open a low door. "In you go," he said. "All the old photographs are piled up in that trunk over there. I am afraid they are not in any sort of order."

"Don't worry." Agatha knelt down by the trunk. "We'll manage."

When the vicar had left, she opened the trunk and let

out a groan. "Hundreds of them. You take a pile out, Toni, and I'll start on another pile."

They worked in silence. It had usually been a very small affair indeed. Agatha found a photograph of George standing with two women. One was recognizable as Sybilla. The other, she supposed, must be George's late wife, Sarah. Sarah Selby was less attractive than Agatha had imagined her to be. She was small with a neat figure, but her hair was a mousy colour and her dress was a print one with an ugly fussy design on it. Sybilla was gazing up at George adoringly. Agatha was about to put the picture down and reach for another when something caught her eye. She fished in her handbag and took out a magnifying glass. Toni giggled. "I didn't think real-life detectives used those."

"Never mind. Come here and look at this." Toni peered at the photograph. "There, in the background, behind those three, that's Maggie Tubby and just look at the expression on her face. Now which one of the three do you think she hates so much?"

"That's interesting, but hardly proof of anything," said Toni. "Let's go on looking for something else, or there might be other photos of Maggie."

"Oh, here's another wedding at the church and Maggie again," exclaimed Toni. "Take a look at this one. There! In the background on the left side."

"Well, I'll be damned!" Agatha peered at the

photograph. Maggie was standing at the side gazing up at George.

"Now, surely that's the look of a woman in love," said Toni. "I thought she was a lesbian."

"Never mind about that. These days, if a woman lives with another woman, particularly in a small village, then they're judged to be a pair of lesbians." Agatha scowled. "I'd like to show her this, just to see her reaction. I wonder if there is a way of getting her on her own. I also wonder why she was so anxious to say that George had worked up Sybilla to killing his wife."

"We can hardly stalk her in a small village like this," said Toni. "Is there a village shop here?"

"Didn't notice one. Did you?"

"No. So that means they'll need to go into Mircester to do their shopping. People do go shopping on Sunday. We could go up out of the village and find a secluded bit to conceal the car and see if she drives past. Or if Phyllis leaves, then we can go back to the village and see Maggie on her own."

"Right," said Agatha. "We'll try that and just hope that precious pair don't decide to go shopping together. We better drive past their cottage and see what sort of car they drive."

Agatha reversed up a road in a lane leading up to a farm and parked under the shelter of a stand of trees. "So we're looking for one of those old Volvo estate cars, built like a hearse."

After half an hour of watching and waiting, Toni said, "This is going to be difficult. Everyone from the village who's passed us must have been driving at sixty miles an hour."

"There she goes!" howled Agatha as a glimpse of a grey Volvo flashed past. They set off in pursuit.

"Can you see who's driving?" asked Toni.

"I'm sure it's Maggie. She's smaller than Phyllis."

"Don't get too close! You don't want her to see us!" cried Toni.

"I am not getting too close," said Agatha through gritted teeth. She did not like the feeling of taking orders from Toni. But she held back when they reached the main road and let two cars get in front of her.

Maggie—and with any luck it was Maggie, thought Agatha—drove into the main car park in Mircester. "I'll look," said Toni after Agatha had parked some distance away. She jumped out of the car and after about a minute came racing back. "It's her."

"You'd better follow her," said Agatha reluctantly. "She would spot me a mile off. Tell me if she goes into a restaurant or goes to the supermarket. Then come back quickly."

Agatha lit a cigarette while she waited, wondering as she often did if she would ever give up smoking, or if something awful like cancer would make up her mind for her.

Toni seemed to be gone a long time, but she was away only ten minutes before she came flying back.

"Well?" demanded Agatha.

"You'll never believe this."

"Believe what?"

"Maggie went into that Chinese restaurant and George Selby was already there. I looked through the window. He got up to meet her and kissed her full on the mouth!"

"Now, there's a thing," said Agatha. "I wonder if Maggie has a lot of money. I know she sells expensive pottery, but maybe she's got family money. Yet it was Maggie who suggested that Sybilla might have murdered Sarah because of her infatuation with George."

"George might have heard the rumours she's putting around and is trying to smooch her out of any such ideas," suggested Toni.

"I know," said Agatha. "Let's go and call on Phyllis. I'll ask her if George is interested in women with money and tell her about my date with him. I'll be blunt."

As usual, thought Toni. But she said aloud, "I didn't know you'd had a date with George."

"It might have ended up something warmer if Charles hadn't been at my cottage when I got home. Now I think of it, George might have been courting me because he thought I was rich."

As she said those last words, Agatha felt a darkness settle somewhere in the region of her stomach. She didn't want to believe the truth of what she had just said, and yet she had to admit, sadly, it was possible, particularly when she set herself against the glowing youth of Toni.

"Get in the car," she ordered gruffly.

Not receiving any reply when they rang the front doorbell, Agatha and Toni made their way round the side of the cottage to the back. Phyllis was sprawled out on an old green canvas deck chair in her back garden.

She did not get to her feet when she saw them but smiled lazily up at them and asked, "What is it now?"

"It's about Maggie," said Agatha.

Phyllis's catlike features hardened. "If you want to know anything about Maggie, ask her. She's gone into Mircester to do some shopping, but she should be back later this afternoon."

"Maggie is in Mircester, yes, but having a romantic lunch with George Selby," said Agatha.

For one brief moment, Phyllis's face registered shock. She quickly regained her composure and said, "Why not? What business is it of yours?"

"George came on to me," said Agatha, "and I think his motive was because I am a rich woman."

Phyllis's eyes raked Agatha up and down. "It could hardly be anything else," she said sweetly. Her gaze fell on Toni, who was wearing a crop top and shorts, showing an expanse of slightly tanned midriff and long smooth legs. "Now, if you had a figure like that—"

"Take this seriously," snapped Agatha. "Does Maggie have money?"

"She does. But why should that interest George Selby?"

"Look at it this way. You said Sybilla was dotty about George. Perhaps he encouraged her to push his wife down the stairs. Now he's after Maggie."

"Get out of here!" said Phyllis. "You're only cross because you didn't even get to first base with George. You're jealous!"

"Don't say I didn't warn you," said Agatha. "Come on, Toni."

"Now what?" asked Toni when they were outside the cottage.

"That garden of theirs backs onto a field," said Agatha. "I wonder if we could get into that field. I would like to listen to what happens between that pair when Maggie gets back."

"Difficult," said Toni. "I'm sure we've already set the lace curtains in this village twitching. How do we get round the back without anyone noticing?"

Agatha scowled in thought. "I know," she said. "We could drive up to the manor house and go through the grounds and make our way across the fields from there."

"Maggie'll be a while yet. Can we go somewhere and

buy some sandwiches and drinks to take with us?" asked Toni.

"Good idea."

By the time they had made their way across the fields carrying a bag of sandwiches and drinks, Agatha felt hot and tired. Fortunately the cottage gardens were screened by trees and bushes.

"How will we know which garden is Phyllis's?" asked Toni.

"It's the one with the big cedar tree against the fence," said Agatha. "I'm dying to sit down and have a cigarette."

"You can't!" protested Toni.

"Why? Have you joined the ranks of people who persecute smokers?"

"No, it's just that there isn't even a breeze and Phyllis could smell cigarette smoke and decide to investigate."

"Good point. It's all right. I don't need to smoke," said Agatha defiantly, but thinking longingly of the packet of twenty in her handbag.

They found the back of Phyllis's garden and settled down on the grass at the edge of the field to wait. They couldn't talk in case Phyllis heard them. They ate sandwiches as quietly as they could and drank mineral water.

As the afternoon dragged on, Agatha fell asleep. She dreamed that she was passionately in love with James Lacey once more. Once more all her senses were alive and her life full of excitement. Then she was dragged out of her highly coloured dream by Toni shaking her awake.

"Maggie's back," whispered Toni.

They strained their ears.

At first all they could hear were faint sounds of some altercation. Then the voices grew louder as Maggie and Phyllis moved into the garden.

"I'm asking you again," came Phyllis's voice. "Why didn't you tell me?"

"You never liked George."

"No, and I thought you didn't either. You were always saying there was something fishy about Sarah's death. Anyway, I had that infuriating woman, Agatha Raisin, round here warning me that George was only after your money."

"What!"

"Said he made a pass at her."

"Rubbish!"

"She is rather sexy, you know."

"Nonsense!"

"Then dear George's interest in her must have been because of the money."

Maggie said, "He got a terrific whack from Sarah's insurance."

"I happen to know," said Phyllis coldly, "that he didn't get a penny. He had let her life insurance lapse."

"Why didn't you tell me?" shrieked Maggie this time.

"I didn't want you to know that he had taken *me* out for a romantic dinner about a month ago. You were always saying that you didn't like him. He said we both seemed comfortably off. That's when I told him you had all the money and I hardly had a bean. Up to that point, he had been quite flirtatious. The minute I told him about not having money, he looked just as if someone had thrown a bucket of cold water over him. I never found out why he was so desperate for money. Did you?"

"No," said Maggie, sounding suddenly weary. "I knew you wouldn't like it, so I only pretended to think he caused his wife's death. I've got to go inside. I didn't put the milk and cheese in the fridge."

Agatha signalled to Toni that they should leave. Toni rose up in one single fluid movement while Agatha struggled to her feet, ignoring that warning twinge in her hip. They made their way wearily back to the car.

Agatha drove up out of the village and then stopped at the side of the road. "What do you make of that?"

"I wonder why he so desperately needs money," said Toni. "Maybe we should be following him."

"Good idea. I feel whatever he's up to happens in the evening. Give Mrs. Freedman details of your overtime."

———

When Toni checked her phone that evening, there was a text from Harry. "Please phone. Going on holiday tomorrow." She nervously bit her thumb. The grown-up thing would be to phone. "But I'm not grown up," said Toni aloud, "and I don't want to phone him." She switched off her mobile and decided not to check it for messages until the following day, when she hoped Harry would be safely on his way somewhere for his holiday.

Early the following evening, Toni and Agatha set out to park in the same place where they had lurked to watch for Maggie leaving the village. "He drives a black BMW," said Agatha. "It's going to be difficult to spot a black car racing past."

"I know," said Toni, "I'll go down to the road and hide behind one of those trees. When I spot him, I'll run back."

Agatha waited impatiently. She lit a cigarette, took a few puffs and then put it out. She had been momentarily cheered by a new item on television about a hundred-year-old woman who had smoked since the age of seven, but was then depressed when the old lady said she smoked only four cigarettes a day and didn't inhale.

Just as it was beginning to get dark, Toni hurtled back to the car, crying out, "He's just gone past."

Agatha set off in pursuit.

After several miles, straining their eyes to try to keep him in view, George turned onto the Oxford Road.

"It's so hard to see with all these cars," complained Agatha as they approached Oxford.

"I see him," said Toni. "He's taken the roundabout. Must be going into Oxford by the Woodstock Road."

"Unless he's going in to London," said Agatha.

But on the Woodstock Road, where the traffic slowed down to thirty miles an hour under the harsh glare of the sodium lights, they could clearly see George's car. At last he turned off on Clarendon Street and went along Walton Street a little way and then parked. Agatha carefully parked several cars behind him.

He turned down Aurelius Street, went up to the door of a trim villa and rang the bell. A statuesque blonde promptly answered the door and fell into his arms. The couple engaged in a passionate clinch.

"I wonder who she is," said Agatha. She and Toni had cautiously followed on foot. "We can hardly stand out in the street waiting to see what happens. We'll go back and wait in the car."

They waited and waited. At one point Toni went off to a fish-and-chip shop and came back with their supper. By the time the bells of Oxford were chiming out midnight, there was still no sign of George.

Agatha yawned and stretched. "I think we should check into a hotel for the night and then come back, say, about seven. This is only two-hour parking, so he'll want to collect his car before the traffic wardens start checking in the morning."

To Toni's relief, Agatha booked them into two single rooms at a hotel up by the roundabout. She wanted to wash out her underwear for the morning and somehow did not want to endure the intimacy of stripping off in front of Agatha.

They set out again at six-thirty the following morning. To Agatha's relief, George's car was still there.

At quarter past seven, George appeared, hurrying towards his car. He jumped in and drove off. "Don't we follow him?" asked Toni.

"No, we put some more money in the parking meter and then go to the end of the road and keep a watch on that house. I want to find out who she is and where she goes."

It was another long wait. At last, just before nine, the blonde came out and got into her car, a small Ford Escort, and drove off. Agatha groaned as, followed by Toni, she rushed back to her own car and set off in pursuit.

"Thank goodness her car is red," said Agatha. "I wonder where she's going. She's heading towards Woodstock. Oh, look, now she's turning off. I know, there's an expensive health farm along this road. It's called Bartley's. I've often thought of going there for a weekend. She doesn't know us, so we can follow her right in, if that's where she's going."

Sure enough, the blonde turned in at the gates of the health farm. "Right," said Agatha, when they saw her enter the building. "We'll give it a few moments and then go in and ask for a tour of the place."

In answer to Agatha's query, the receptionist said their public relations officer would be glad to take them around and show them the facilities. Agatha stifled a yawn as they moved from treatment room to treatment room and then studied health food menus. Then Agatha caught a glimpse of George's blonde, now dressed in a white overall, going into one of the rooms. "Who is that?" she asked. "I think I've seen her somewhere before."

"Oh, that's Gilda Brenson, one of our masseuses."

"No, I don't know her. But is she good?"

"The best. But I fear we might soon be losing her. Gilda is getting married and her future husband is going to set her up in a clinic of her own. Now, if you will just follow me, I will show you our gym . . ."

At the end of the tour, Agatha said brightly, "It all looks splendid. I shall probably book in for a week before

Christmas. But I wonder if I could ask a favour? I really could do with a massage. I would gladly pay you for Gilda's services if she has a free appointment this morning."

"Come to the reception desk with me and I'll see what we can do."

The receptionist said that Gilda would be free in half an hour, so Agatha and Toni settled down to wait.

Agatha saw a reflection of herself in a mirror opposite where they were sitting. Her skirt was creased and she had a ladder in one leg of her tights. Beside her reflection, Toni glowed with youth and health.

At last, Agatha was ushered into the massage room and told to remove her clothes and lie on the massage table. She winced as she climbed on.

"Trouble with your hip?" asked Gilda.

"No," said Agatha defiantly. "Nothing up with me at all." She did not want to admit to having arthritis even to herself.

Gilda was indeed good at her job. Agatha nearly fell asleep but remembered in time why she was there.

"I hear you will shortly be leaving," said Agatha.

"Yes. I am going to be married and then my fiancé says he will set me up in a clinic of my own. There is a good location near the centre of Oxford."

"That will be expensive," commented Agatha. "You are lucky to be marrying such a rich man. What does he do for a living?"

"He is a very successful architect."

"Have you known him a long time?"

"For a few years. He wanted to marry me before, but I always refused. I told him, I need a business of my own for security."

Agatha fell silent, her brain whirring. Why was George courting rich women? Did he plan to get them so enamoured with him that they would invest in this clinic? A few years? Was he courting her while his wife was alive? She decided she must try to secure another date with George and see if he suggested anything like that. She did not want to ask Gilda any more questions in case she became suspicious. Agatha knew she would have to pay by credit card. She did not have enough cash with her. She could only hope Gilda would not be curious enough to ask at reception for her name. Fortunately, in booking her in, the receptionist had not asked for her name because it was an on-the-spot arrangement.

After the session was over, Agatha paid at the desk and then reluctantly asked Toni to drive her back to Mircester because she was feeling exhausted.

Toni said she was happy to go to work for the rest of the day. Agatha lied and said she had something to check up on, all the while planning to head straight home and go to bed.

When she awoke, she decided to try to get in touch with George.

———

George Selby sounded at first surprised and then delighted when Agatha invited him out to dinner that evening.

Agatha had chosen Mircester's most expensive restaurant, Henri's, for dinner. She hoped the atmosphere of discreet lighting and tables set well apart would set the scene for an intimate conversation, and she cynically guessed that the price of the dishes on the menu would endear her to George.

She brushed her thick brown hair until it shone and made up her face carefully. The evening was not warm enough for a summer dress, so she chose to wear one of rich gold fine jersey, flattering to her figure.

Agatha drove wearing flat heels, changed into a pair of stilettos in Mircester car park and tottered towards the restaurant.

George was already there, and her heart gave a treacherous little flutter when she saw him. She hoped he would turn out to be a really fine person after all. He was wearing a beautifully tailored dark suit, white shirt, and silk tie. Those magnetic green eyes of his lit up when he saw her.

"Your invitation came as a nice surprise," he said when she sat down. "You are looking very well. What's this in aid of?"

Agatha fluttered false eyelashes, hoping they would

not fall off. "I should have thought asking a handsome man to dinner would not need any explanation," she said. "Do choose something nice to eat."

"Shall I choose for both of us?"

Something unholy flickered across Agatha's bearlike eyes and then she forced a smile.

"Go ahead."

As she had expected, he started to order the most expensive items on the menu—a dozen oysters each to begin, followed by tournedos Rossini. He ordered a bottle of white wine to go with the oysters and a vintage claret to accompany the steak.

"Now, do tell me about yourself," said Agatha. "We've never really had a chance to talk properly. I'm afraid that last time I did all the talking."

"Oh, business is very successful," said George. "I've been working hard."

"I find clever investment is a good idea," said Agatha. "I mean, it is better to use money to make money rather than leaving it to just lie in the bank."

"Exactly!" beamed George. "Here are our oysters."

Agatha fortunately liked oysters, but she could have sworn that George did not. She guessed he was eating them because he thought it the sophisticated thing to do. He was certainly washing them down with a large amount of wine, which suited Agatha, who wanted to keep a clear head. She suddenly wondered if he came from a poor background.

"You were talking about investments," said George. He had swallowed the last of his oysters with a look on his face reminiscent of a child taking medicine.

"Yes."

"I have something that might interest you."

"Do go on."

"I have a friend who is starting her own beauty salon in Oxford." George leaned his elbows on the table, his eyes fixed on Agatha's face. "The thing is this. Beauty salons used to be only for the rich, but now there is more money around, all sorts of ordinary people want massage, tanning and non-surgical facelifts. It can't fail."

"Sounds good. What is the name of this friend?"

"Why?"

"Simple question."

"Gilda Brenson."

"So what is she selling? Shares? If it's not up and running, she can hardly have floated the salon as a company on the stock market."

"No, the offer would be this. You would get two per cent of the net profits."

"Now, that's not good. I would only be interested in two per cent of the gross. How much would you want me to invest?"

George took a deep breath. He leaned across the table and took Agatha's hand in his. The tournedos arrived. George scowled. "This came too quickly," he said. "I don't like it when it comes too quickly. It looks as if it's been precooked and just waiting in the kitchen."

"Looks great to me," said Agatha cheerfully. "Why don't we eat it first and discuss businesses afterwards? And I can't eat while you're holding my hand."

"Oh, right."

George proceeded to eat and drink quickly. Between bites, Agatha talked about the weather and the disastrous results of the flooding. When she had finished eating and had embarked on yet another flooding story, George interrupted her by asking eagerly, "So, you would be interested?"

"In what?"

"In investing in this salon?"

"Would you care for dessert?" asked the waiter.

"Go away and give us a break," snapped George. He turned his gaze back on Agatha. "Well?"

"How much?" asked Agatha.

"Oh, nothing much. Seventy-five thousand pounds."

"That is actually a lot of money."

"Come on, Agatha. It's a great chance for you to make money." Again he took her hand. "I can see a future for us," he breathed.

"Together?"

"Why not?"

"And what would Gilda have to say about us being together?"

"Agatha, Agatha, my darling. Poor old Gilda is just a business associate."

Agatha withdrew her hand and leaned back in her chair. "Gilda is your fiancée, is she not?"

His mouth fell open.

"You've a bit of puréed spinach on your teeth," commented Agatha. "It matches your eyes."

He scrubbed his front teeth furiously with his napkin. "How did you know Gilda was my fiancée?"

"I'm a detective. I detect. And you interest me an awful lot. I think you're in debt and the fair Gilda won't marry you until you produce the goods. Did you get Sybilla to push your wife downstairs?"

Agatha had read in books of people's faces going black with fury. Now she knew what the writers meant.

"No, I did not murder my wife," hissed George. "You are a malicious old trout."

"Now we've settled that," said Agatha. "What about pudding?"

"Screw the pudding and you!"

George thrust his chair back, stood up and stormed out of the restaurant.

I might have done something dangerous, thought Agatha and called for the bill.

———

When she entered her cottage, carrying her stiletto shoes, she found Charles in the living room, sitting with her cats and watching television.

"Hot date?" asked Charles lazily. "Those eyelashes are a bit much."

"I've been out for dinner with George Selby. Let me tell you what's been going on."

Charles switched off the television and listened carefully. When Agatha had finished, Charles said, "How could you do such a stupid thing? If the man really is a murderer, he'll come after you."

"It's a risk I have to take," said Agatha. "Aren't looks so misleading? I don't think he'll come after me. Too obvious."

"If he charmed Sybilla into bumping off his wife, he may get this Gilda to drop by one night and strangle you."

"Now I'm at dead slow and stop," said Agatha, sinking down on the sofa beside him.

"What are all those boxes of photos doing on the floor?"

"I phoned Toni before I went to sleep today and told her to go back to the vicarage and collect them. We didn't really have time to look at them thoroughly."

"What are you looking for?"

"Someone in former photos whose face doesn't fit."

"Aha! Some sinister face holding a dagger."

"Something like that."

"So you don't think it's a local?"

"Not any more. I can't think any of them would do it. I'm going to bed."

"What's the programme for tomorrow?"

"Office, I suppose. What about you?"

"I feel like a lazy day. I'll take a look at those photos for you. Did you find anything during the first search?"

"Yes. Maggie Tubby is in one of them, gazing adoringly at George. She's got money. He took her for lunch yesterday and gave her a passionate kiss. I know what I'll do tomorrow. I'll pay a call on Maggie and tell her about George's fiancée."

"If she's promised to invest money and you make her pull back, then dear George is really going to feel murderous. I'll come with you."

Chapter Nine

S HE MAY HAVE PULLED OUT ALREADY," said Agatha as she parked in front of Maggie's cottage. "I told Phyllis George had already been romancing me, went and listened outside their back garden and learned that George had previously tried his scam on with Phyllis and that's when she told him Maggie had the money."

"Let's see the reaction anyway," said Charles. "She's probably still in love with him."

"Why?"

"Obsession dies hard, doesn't it, Aggie? Heard from James?"

"Do shut up and ring the bell."

Maggie herself answered the door. "What is it now?" she demanded.

"May we come in?" asked Agatha.

"No."

"Well, I may as well shout it on the doorstep. It's about George."

Maggie hesitated. Then she said reluctantly, "Come in, but just for a moment."

They followed her through to her shed in the garden. "I was working," said Maggie. She turned and faced them outside the shed door. "What is it?"

"I've found out that George Selby is engaged to a certain masseuse called Gilda Brenson. She won't marry him unless he buys her a clinic in Oxford, so he's been trying to get money out of us to fund it."

Maggie put out a hand and leaned on the shed door. Her normally rosy cheeks had turned pale.

"It can't be true."

"I'm afraid it is. Did you give him any money?"

"Two hundred thousand," said Maggie in a hoarse whisper. "He promised to marry me. I'll kill him."

"Don't do that," said Charles. "There's been enough killing already."

"Why don't you tell the vicar about it?" suggested Agatha. "It may be that George has tried to get his hands on some of the money from the fête."

"Just leave," said Maggie. "Leave now."

Toni received a text from Harry. "In Turkey. Back in week. Want to see u."

Steeling herself, Toni texted back, "Don't want see u. Got boyfriend."

And I hope that's that, she thought.

Her doorbell rang. At least it can't be Harry, thought Toni, going to answer it. It was her friend Sharon.

"Feel like going to see the Living Legends?" she asked.

"I thought you were going with Simon." Simon was Sharon's boyfriend.

"He's dumped me, that's what."

"Never!"

"Yeah. Got me to get tickets and then told me he was going with Cheryl, her with the big boobs and the nose ring."

"I'll go with you," said Toni, thinking that a pop concert might be a good antidote to the feelings of inadequacy engendered in her by Harry.

While Charles went back to Agatha's cottage to look at the old photographs, Agatha went to her office to find a local reporter, Harriet Winry, waiting for her. Harriet was a thin, bespectacled girl with bad skin and lank hair. What she lacked in looks she made up for with enthusiasm for her job.

"Nothing to report," said Agatha curtly. "Get out of here. I've got work to do."

"What about that business at Comfrey Magna?" asked Harriet.

"Still investigating. Now, go away . . . Wait a minute. I might have a little bit of news for you, nothing much."

"What is it?"

"Handsome widower George Selby is engaged to gorgeous masseuse Gilda Brenson. Not much, but it'd make a nice item for the local gossip column. A photo of Gilda might be worth it. She is very glamorous. Works at Bartley's Health Farm. She'll be leaving shortly because George is going to set her up with her own salon. To this end, he's been begging his wealthy female friends to invest in the salon."

"Thanks, Agatha. Might make a nice little piece."

Agatha grinned. "Just what I thought."

Harriet left and Phil Marshall arrived carrying his camera bag. "I think I've got enough on that divorce case," he said. "What now?"

"We'd better get over to Herry's shoe factory. They say someone's been pinching their designs and they want us to investigate."

The managing director of the shoe company, Jimmy Binter, talked to them in the boardroom. "It's the second time Comfort Shoes has stolen our designs. We do a line which specializes in wide fittings."

"When did the first one happen?" asked Agatha

"Last spring. One of our models appeared in their spring catalogue, and now another of our latest models is featured in their autumn catalogue."

"How many do you employ?"

"It's a small company. Forty on the work force, two designers and four salesmen."

"I need a list of their names."

"I have it right here."

Agatha studied the list and then said, "Mark off the names who started work before, say, last November."

"I'll call our personnel manager, Mrs. Goody. She'll help you."

"Where is the catalogue printed?"

"At Jones Printers in Mircester. But whoever stole the designs for the shoes wouldn't work at the printer's. The shoe featured in the spring catalogue was copied exactly. Someone would need the original design."

Mrs. Goody arrived and ticked off the names and addresses of the employees who had started work last autumn.

Agatha busily took notes and then stood up. "I'll get back to you. Give me a spring and an autumn catalogue."

Outside the factory, Phil said, "What do you plan to do?"

"There's a new designer, Carry Wilks, taken on last year. She's our best bet. Let's check where she lives. If she lives with her parents, it'll slow things up. But if I remember rightly, it's block of flats, one of those tower blocks out on the Evesham road."

Agatha drove steadily, smoking and blowing smoke around the car. Phil coughed crossly and opened a window.

"Here we are," said Agatha. "She lives in number thirty-four. I hope it isn't too high up because often the lifts in these places are broken."

The lift was, indeed, broken. Agatha felt her hip getting worse as she mounted the smelly stone staircase. Phil seemed to take the stairs as easily as a teenager.

"Here we are, thirty-four." Agatha rang the bell. A child wailed from a nearby apartment and a rising wind moaned around the building.

"No reply. Let's see if we can get in." Agatha took out a credit card.

"You can't!" protested Phil. "That's breaking and entering."

"It's just a Yale lock," said Agatha, ignoring him. "Good heavens! It works. I thought maybe that only worked in the movies. Come in and shut the door behind you."

The flat appeared to consist of a small living room, bedroom, tiny kitchen and a shower. Agatha went over to a desk by the window and began to search after putting on a pair of latex gloves.

"Nothing here," she said while Phil waited nervously. "I could try this computer."

"Probably protected by a password," said Phil.

"May not be." Agatha switched it on. "Let me see. E-mail. No, I can get right into it. Bingo. Silly cow. Here it is. 'I'll be bringing over the designs and expect the usual fee,' sent to Comfort Shoes."

"But we can't do anything with this evidence," protested Phil. "We can't say how we got it."

"Never mind. Back to the factory, and watch me!"

The managing director summoned Carry Wilks. A tall, mannish-looking woman came into the boardroom.

Agatha got straight to the point. "You've been selling designs to Comfort Shoes. There's been a leak at their factory. You corresponded with them via e-mail."

"What have you got to say for yourself?" demanded the managing director.

"Just this," said Carry. "Screw the lot of you." She marched out of the boardroom.

The managing director called for security to stop Carry from leaving the building. "I got the information by breaking into her flat," said Agatha, "so call the police and get them to search her place and don't say anything about me. Get her charged first. Say you got a tip-off from an anonymous caller at Comfort Shoes."

As Agatha drove off, a police car sped past, heading for the factory. "I'm glad there weren't any children," said Agatha. "I mean, if she had been a single mother with kids to support, I might have felt bad about turning her in."

When Agatha got back to her cottage that evening, she found Charles had left her a note. "Got to go home.

Have taken the photos with me. May be back tonight. Love, Charles."

Agatha sat down at the kitchen table after having let her cats out into the garden. She was just about to go through the morning's mail, which she had not had time to open, when the phone rang. It was Roy Silver. "Are you all right?" he asked.

"Sure. Why?"

There was a silence and Roy said, "I think I should come down for the weekend."

"You're welcome. Any particular reason?"

"We're friends."

"Okay. I'll pick you up at Moreton Station, usual time, around six-thirty in the evening."

"See you then."

What's up with him? Agatha wondered.

Ever since the advent of e-mail, one hardly ever got anything interesting in the post, apart from bills and junk mail. Agatha put the junk mail on one side to be thrown away and the bills on the other side. There was an interesting-looking square envelope of expensive paper. Agatha saved it for last and then slit it open and drew out a heavily embossed invitation.

At first she could hardly believe what she was reading. She rose stiffly from the kitchen table, went through to the living room and poured herself a gin and tonic. Returning to the kitchen table, she lit a cigarette, took a good strong pull of her drink and studied the invitation again. It said:

Mrs. Agatha Raisin
and the staff of the Agatha Raisin Detective Agency
are invited to a reception
at the George Hotel, Mircester, on October 2nd
to celebrate the engagement
of Felicity Jane Bross-Tilkington
to Mr. James Bartholomew Lacey.
Drinks and snacks. Dress informal.
Reception at 7:30 P.M. in the Betjeman Suite.
RSVP Mrs. Olivia Bross-Tilkington,
The Laurels, Downboys, Sussex, SX12 5JW

Agatha felt her heart thumping against her ribs. When had all this happened? He had written to her a month ago and said nothing about it.

She heard her front door opening and Charles calling, "Anybody home?"

"In the kitchen," said Agatha, thrusting the invitation under the pile of junk mail.

Charles came in carrying the boxes of photographs. "You have a look. I can't find anything. Yes, I got an invitation as well and from the lost look in your eyes, so did you."

"Bastard!" said Agatha. "Why didn't he tell me?"

"Why should he? All was over between the two of you. Stop being bitch in the manger and look forward to the evening. It'll be interesting to see who won that confirmed bachelor's heart."

"I don't expect you to understand," said Agatha stiffly.

"Oh, but I do. You don't want him, but you don't want anyone else to have him."

"He should have told me!" howled Agatha.

"So you keep saying. Drop it. Life goes on."

"I won't go."

"Of course you will."

"He's invited the whole bloody agency."

"And you were thinking of not telling anybody?"

Agatha scowled. "Something like that."

"You'll just have to be a big girl and go. Wish him well. Be a lady."

"Oh, all right. That must be why Roy is coming down this weekend. He must have had an invitation as well. Probably thinks my hand needs holding."

"That's what friends are for. Are you any further forward with finding out who put acid in the jam?"

"Not a clue. But I'm beginning to wonder a lot about George Selby."

"You've spiked his guns. He'll probably move to another village and start all over again. Now, I'd better be going. I just came back to give you the photographs."

"Can't you stay for a meal?"

"One of your frozen curries? No, thanks. Probably be around later in the week."

The following day Agatha worked hard, because there was a backlog of unsolved cases. By the time she finished up, it was seven o'clock. She bought a copy of the Mircester newspaper before driving home. Once she had fussed over her cats and settled down at the kitchen table, she opened the newspaper and scanned the items. On page seven, there was a photo of Gilda posed outside the health farm, looking very glamorous. The headline was, "Architect Needs Money Before He Can Wed." The story said that local architect George Selby was pleading with rich friends to put money into his glamorous fiancée's venture of opening up her own clinic; otherwise she would not marry him. "'I think he will get the necessary money,' said beautiful Gilda Brenson yesterday. 'He knows I must have my own business before I marry. Careers last, men don't.'" The story went on to say that Mr. Selby lived in Comfrey Magna, scene of that disastrous fête where two women met their death after sampling jam heavily laced with LSD. It ended by saying that Mr. George Selby was unavailable for comment.

"I bet he is," muttered Agatha.

There was a ring at the doorbell. Agatha got wearily to her feet and clutched her hip. She didn't want a hip replacement. Not yet, surely. So ageing. She opened the door.

A furious George Selby thrust her into the hall. "You horrible old bat!" he yelled. "You got that story in the local rag." He had Agatha by the shoulders and was shaking her.

"Are you going to k-kill m-me the w-way you k-killed your w-wife?" shouted Agatha.

He drew back his fist and punched her hard on the face. "I could kill *you*."

Mrs. Bloxby, finding the door opened, had just walked in, clutching a jar of home-made chutney. She rushed forward and brought the jar down on George's head and he slumped to the floor.

"Mrs. Raisin! Are you all right?"

"Thanks to you."

Mrs. Bloxby knelt down by George. "Call an ambulance."

"I'm calling the police as well," said Agatha.

After what seemed an interminable wait, George was borne off in an ambulance. Two policemen had arrived and were taking notes. One turned to Mrs. Bloxby. "You are to come to the station with us and we caution you that anything—"

"What? Why?" screamed Agatha.

"We are charging you with causing grievous bodily harm."

"You're mad. She saved my life!" shouted Agatha and burst into tears.

Wilkes was furious when he learned the news. He knew officers were under constant pressure by the government to meet targets, but he knew the scandal the arrest of Mrs. Bloxby would cause. He had to interrupt Agatha, who was holding a press conference outside the police station about the iniquities of the force, to announce that no charges were being brought against Mrs. Bloxby. He warned Agatha not to say anything about it as, when George Selby recovered from what turned out to be a straightforward concussion, he would be put on trial.

But there was nothing he could do to stop the press from taking pictures of Mrs. Bloxby as she emerged from police headquarters. Bill Wong drove them both back to Carsely. Wearily, Agatha told him all about George's engagement and how he had been trying to get money to fund Gilda's clinic.

"Leave it alone," urged Bill when she had finished. "I don't think we'll ever know whether he conspired with Sybilla to kill his wife, but I don't really see what we can do about it now."

"Is Mr. Selby going to be all right?" asked Mrs. Bloxby nervously.

"Yes. By the time the ambulance had got him to hospital, he was conscious and phoning his lawyer. You're a brave woman. Agatha, are you sure you shouldn't have gone to hospital for a check-up? There's a huge bruise coming up on your cheek."

"I'm fine."

Bill wondered whether to mention that he had received an invitation to James's engagement party and then decided against it.

When they arrived at Agatha's cottage, Bill offered to drive Mrs. Bloxby on to the vicarage, but she refused, saying she wanted to talk to Agatha.

"I'll be off, then," said Bill. "We're friends, right, Agatha? So if you need a shoulder to cry on, I'm always there for you."

"What would I want to cry about?" said Agatha defiantly. "My face isn't that sore."

When Bill had driven off, Mrs. Bloxby followed Agatha into her cottage. "The police took away the chutney," she said. "Good glass. It didn't even break. Let me make you a cup of tea."

"I'd like a stiff brandy."

"Hot sweet tea is better for shock."

"Brandy is for forgetting. I'll get it. What about you?"

"A sherry would be nice."

"Now," said Mrs. Bloxby, after she had taken a little sip of sherry, "I received an invitation today to Mr. Lacey's engagement party."

"Oh, I knew all about that," said Agatha airily.

Mrs. Bloxby studied her friend's face.

Agatha crumpled. "Well, actually I didn't know. And, yes, it was a shock."

"But you didn't want him any more."

"I know. But I'm getting on and . . . and . . . as long as I thought he still wanted me, it meant there was someone out there who did. I can't stand the idea of everyone pitying me and thinking I'll be in mourning. I hate being pitied!"

"No one will pity you if you turn up at that party and give him your blessing."

"I rather thought of not going."

"Then everyone *will* pity you."

"Snakes and bastards!" Agatha let out a puff of angry cigarette smoke and took a gulp of brandy. "I wonder what she's like?"

"There's only one way to find out. Go."

"I suppose so. I wonder why. I mean, he always struck me as a confirmed bachelor. Even when we were married, he went on as if I were some sort of junior officer. Look, thank you so much for saving me. I wonder if George really would have killed me?"

"He's a dangerous man," said Mrs. Bloxby with a shudder. "I'd better get back to the vicarage."

As she walked through the hall, Mrs. Bloxby said, "A bit of the jar must have broken after all. Look! There's a bit of glass on the floor." She bent down and picked it up. "It's a contact lens, a green contact lens."

Agatha grinned. "So much for George's beautiful green eyes."

When Agatha met Roy as he arrived by train on Friday, she had to endure being clasped to his thin bosom. "You poor, poor darling," said Roy.

"Get off me!" snarled Agatha. "If you think I am in mourning over James's engagement, forget about it."

"There's no need to be so rude," retorted Roy angrily. "Really, sweetie, it's a wonder you've got any friends left, the way you go on."

"I can't stand the idea of everyone being sorry for me," said Agatha. "I'm sorry I snapped at you. Come along. I'll take you for dinner."

Roy was dressed conservatively in a dark suit, white shirt and striped silk tie. "Sticky account?" asked Agatha sympathetically.

"Very sticky. Jason's Country Clothes. I've to make a big push to promote them."

"Then I would have thought you'd have been kitted out in a Barbour and shooting breeches."

"I was," said Roy as they walked to Agatha's car, his thin face flushed with annoyance. "I even wore a tweed fishing hat and the managing director said I looked ridiculous."

"You weren't wearing your gold earring with the fishing hat, were you?"

"Well, I was. I forgot to take it off. I've got some casuals in my bag."

After they had dined and returned to the cottage, Roy asked, "What are all those boxes of old photos doing on your kitchen table?"

Agatha told him. "I've been through them, and so has Charles."

"I'm not tired," said Roy. "Fix me a coffee and I'll have a look."

Agatha made him a cup of coffee and took herself off to bed. She was awakened an hour later by Roy shaking her. "Leave me alone, Charles," she mumbled.

"It's not him, it's me," said Roy.

Agatha switched on the bedside light and struggled up against the pillows. "What's up? Found something?"

"It's what I haven't found which is interesting."

"That being?"

"It's what's *not* there. There's no photo of the vicar's wedding."

"Well, they'd hardly have it with the rest," complained Agatha. "I bet it's framed in silver somewhere in the vicarage. What did you think? They might not really be married?"

"Something like that."

"Dream on."

"We could nip over there tomorrow. I didn't like Trixie."

"Neither did I. Oh, very well. The vicar might have heard some gossip."

Roy and Agatha set out next morning for Comfrey Magna. Roy was wearing a white silk blouson with skin-tight blue velvet trousers and ankle boots with stacked heels. Agatha reflected that the jeering comment that some man looked like a big girl's blouse could certainly apply to Roy, but she held her tongue. If she criticized his dress, she was sure he would sulk for the rest of the day.

Agatha had phoned the police earlier that morning to say she would not be pressing charges against George. She had no desire to appear in court to be ripped apart in public by some defence counsel.

Arthur Chance opened the door to them himself. "Oh, Mrs. Raisin. Do come in. I am so sorry about Mr. Selby. The poor man must have been terribly over-wrought, but all things end happily."

"Really?" Agatha and Roy followed him in. "How happy?" asked Agatha when they were seated in the vicarage living room.

"Mr. Selby—George—called on me this morning. He checked himself out of hospital. He gave me the glad news."

"That he and Gilda are to be married?"

"That was merely a fabrication of the press. No, he is to be married to Miss Frederica Corrie."

"What! That's sudden."

"Evidently they had been courting for some time."

"And you believe that rubbish?"

"She doesn't want to," came his wife's amused voice. "She's jealous."

"Rubbish," said Agatha. "I'll bet dear Fred is rich."

"Pots of money," said Trixie.

"Well, there's your answer."

"Please leave," said the vicar. "I don't like your unchristian comments. You have brought nothing but tragedy to this village."

"Oh, really? *I* didn't spike the jam. *I* didn't steal the money."

"You heard hubby," said Trixie, her eyes sparkling with malice. "Take your toy boy and shove off."

Agatha opened her mouth to blast her, but Roy pulled at her arm. "Let's just get out of here," he said.

Outside the vicarage, Agatha said, "We're going to see Gilda. I wonder if she knows the news."

They drove to Bartley's Health Farm. "I assume she works on Saturdays," said Agatha. "Wait here. I'll ask at the desk."

After a few minutes," Agatha came hurrying back. "She's at home. I know where she lives."

They drove into Oxford and managed to squeeze into a parking place outside Gilda's house.

Gilda answered the door and stared at Agatha. "So it's you. The private detective. George told me about you."

"Do you know he is engaged to a certain Frederica Corrie?" asked Agatha.

"I am not surprised. I visited him in hospital and told him we were no longer engaged. I have been ridiculed in the press as a gold digger. Now go away."

"What will you do now?"

"Find a really rich man who does not have to chase after silly rich women to get money for me." And with that, Gilda slammed the door in their faces.

"She can't have cared a jot for him," said Agatha as they both got in the car.

"It doesn't solve a thing," complained Roy, "unless you suspect her of having pushed George's wife down the stairs."

"If only I could get a break," mourned Agatha. "Just one little clue."

The Living Legends were holding their pop concert in a manor house field outside Mircester. Young people were flooding in to the event, Toni and Sharon amongst them.

Toni felt elated being surrounded by crowds of her peers. When the band swung into their opening number of "Rock It Hard," she screamed her delight and waved her arms with the rest of the crowd. At the interval, she turned a glowing face to Sharon. "This is great. This is grand, to be among young people. Sometimes I feel like a child at that detective agency."

"They're not all young. Get a look at someone's mummy over there."

Toni's eyes followed Sharon's pointing finger. She let out a little gasp. "You're not going to believe this, but that's the vicar's wife—you know, the one from Comfrey Magna. What's she doing here?"

"Having a rave," said Sharon. "I noticed her during the first half."

The band started up again. This time Toni kept her eyes on Trixie. The vicar's wife was alone. She was wearing a white short-sleeved blouse tied at the waist and very tight jeans and high-heeled boots. She swayed to the music like one possessed.

Then at one point, as if conscious of Toni's gaze on her, Trixie turned and saw her. Sharon grabbed Toni's arm and shouted in her ear, "Aren't you enjoying yourself?"

"Yes," Toni shouted back. She turned back and looked for Trixie, but the vicar's wife had disappeared.

Toni tried to enjoy the rest of the concert, but her mind was racing. At the end, she said to Sharon, "Are they selling drugs here?"

Sharon looked alarmed. "Don't go down that road, Tone."

"No, I just wondered if anyone could buy acid at one of these gigs."

"Heroin, cocaine, skunk, but I don't think acid. Why?"

"I'd better get to Carsely. I've got to tell Agatha about the vicar's wife."

"Oh, forget it. You've got to get some time off."

"I'm sorry, Sharon. I've really got to go. I'll drop you off in Mircester."

Sharon sulked the whole way back into town. But Toni was determined to get this latest piece of news to Agatha.

Agatha was just preparing for bed when the doorbell rang. She wondered whether to answer it in case it was another visit from George. She peered through the spyhole and was relieved to see Toni's face. She opened the door. "What's up? Come in."

In the kitchen, Toni told Agatha about Trixie being at the concert.

Agatha's eyes gleamed. "Was she on her own?"

"Seemed to be. Then she got me looking at her. I turned away and when I turned back, she'd gone."

Roy appeared in the kitchen wrapped in a Chinese silk dressing gown. "What's going on?"

Agatha told him and then said, "We've got to find out her name before she was married. It's probably in the church register. Then we'll need to find out what sort of background she came from."

"The church is open during the day," said Toni, "but we'll need to slip in after the morning service."

"The book'll be in the vestry," said Roy. "I wonder if they keep it locked."

At that moment, Charles wandered in, having let himself into Agatha's cottage with his own set of keys. Agatha looked at his concerned face and said, "No, I am not dead yet. I have more important things to think about."

She told him about Trixie, ending with, "I'd better get Patrick to go. No one knows him."

"There's something else I just remembered," said Toni. "Trixie had these tattoos down her arms."

"You're sure?" Agatha frowned. She had never seen Trixie's arms uncovered. Even the leotard that Trixie had been wearing the first day Agatha had met her had been long-sleeved.

"Did you see what they were like?" asked Roy.

"Yes," said Toni. "Midlands TV was there and they had this white light panning out over the audience. The tattoos were blue, all blue, like ink."

"By all that's holy," breathed Agatha. "Prison tattoos."

Chapter Ten

THE PROBLEM WITH THAT IS," said Toni, "a lot of young people these days have fake prison tattoos."

"Yes, but she's not young," said Agatha. "We must find out what her maiden name was. I'll phone Patrick."

She retreated to the living room. "Aggie's always been determined to make Trixie the villain," said Charles. "I hope she doesn't get too carried away."

Agatha came back saying, "Patrick's going over to the church tomorrow. Now I suggest we all go to bed. Charles, if you're staying, you'll need to sleep on the couch."

"It's all right. I'm going home. I'll drop by tomorrow to see if there's any news."

Agatha slept uneasily, waking several times during the night, worrying about George. She felt he would never forgive her and dreaded that he might try to attack her again. She also worried about Monday morning in the office, when she would need to tell her small staff about the invitation to James's engagement party. Agatha hated to be pitied. She wanted to be feared, admired or loved, but she did not want to be the object of anyone's pity.

Roy was startled at breakfast the following morning when Agatha announced that they were going to church.

"Why?" he wailed. "I don't do church."

"I want to talk to Mrs. Bloxby."

"We could go to the vicarage afterwards."

"I feel guilty about always dropping in on her. Come on. It'll do our souls good."

"I didn't know you had a soul, sweetie."

Agatha was impatient, her mind racing from one thing that needed doing to another. She found the service interminable. She only relaxed during the long sermon, the vicar's words drifting in and out of her brain until she fell asleep and was finally awakened by a sharp nudge in her ribs from Roy's elbow and his voice hissing in her ear, "You're snoring."

After the final hymn and the blessing, they filed out of church. Agatha shook hands with the vicar and said, "Fine sermon. Very moving."

Alf Bloxby replied drily, "But not enough to keep you awake."

"You must be mistaken. I heard every word," lied Agatha. She spotted Mrs. Bloxby talking to some of the parishioners and hurried over to her.

"A word in private," said Agatha, driving off the three women who had been talking to Mrs. Bloxby with a steely glare.

"I hope this is important," said Mrs. Bloxby. "You interrupted me."

"Very important. Do you know anything about Trixie Chance?"

"Until her husband approached me about you publicizing the fête, I did not know anything at all about either Mr. Chance or his wife."

"But you could find out. The clergy gossip to each other."

"Mrs. Raisin, I will only gossip if it is to a good end. What is your motive?"

Agatha told her about the concert and the tattoos. Mrs. Bloxby frowned. "It is all very thin evidence of wrongdoing, but I will see what I can find out."

"Thanks!" Agatha charged off, sweeping Roy with her. "We'd better get back home. Patrick should be calling."

When she got back to her cottage, Agatha checked her answering service. She listened in dismay. Patrick had left a message to say there was no record of the marriage.

Agatha told Roy. "I could go up to London and check at the Records Office," she said, "but it would take ages. Wait! I've an idea. It would be easy if I had an idea of exactly when they got married."

She phoned Toni. "I want to find out when and where the vicar and Trixie got married. That pig farmer fancies you. Would you mind going to Comfrey Magna and asking him?"

"If his wife's around, she'll throw another teapot at me," said Toni, "but, yes, I'll try."

Toni decided to go straight to the pig farm. If Hal's wife was there, she'd just have to beat a retreat.

As she approached the farm, she saw Hal working in a field near the house. She parked the car, vaulted the fence and went to meet him.

"Well, if it isn't the prettiest detective in England," said Hal. "Come to see the pigs?"

"No, I wanted to ask you a question. When did Mr. Chance and his wife get married, and where?"

"Let me see. Must be about ten years ago. We all thought he was a confirmed bachelor. They got married in Moreton Registry Office."

"Not in church?"

"No, there was something about her having been divorced."

"You wouldn't happen to know the date?"

"As a matter of fact, I do. Give us a kiss and I'll tell you."

"Tell me first and I'll give you a kiss," said Toni.

"Okay. I remember because it was the day of the

Moreton Agricultural Show and I got first prize for one of my pigs. That would be on the eighth of September."

"Ten years ago?"

"Right. Now what about that kiss?"

"Another time." Toni darted away, jumped the fence, got into her car and drove off.

Agatha did not want to wait until the council offices in Moreton-in-Marsh opened on Monday morning, only perhaps to find that all records of marriages had been sent up to London. She travelled up on the Sunday night with Roy and booked herself into a hotel for the night, then set off to the records office in Finsbury Park the next day.

Eagerly she filled out the required forms and then searched until she found the right book and searched through the pages. Arthur Chance had married Trixie Webster. Her home address was given as 4A Puddleton Close, Cheltenham.

Agatha phoned Phil and told him to take his cameras over to Comfrey Magna and try to capture a discreet shot of Trixie. Before she went to Cheltenham, Agatha wanted to have a photograph to show around. As she travelled in a taxi back to Paddington Station, she could not lose the feeling that somehow the magic of London for her had disappeared. She could not get over the sensation that the great city had somehow become grimy, dingy and unwelcoming. Maybe it had always been like that, she thought, and one actually had to live in the place to like it once more.

I'm getting countrified, thought Agatha as the train slid out of the station. I have a cottage, I have cats, soon I'll be wearing tweeds. She had always thought of herself as a sophisticated city person, that her stay in the country was perhaps just a phase. She remembered having voiced this idea to Charles, who had said cynically, "Sophisticated City Agatha was just another mask. People do like to glamorize themselves. It saves them from looking at the person they really are."

"And who am I really?" Agatha had demanded angrily.

But Charles had laughed and said, "I wouldn't dare tell you."

Agatha wished she had brought a book or a newspaper to read on the train. There was something unsettling about being left with her own thoughts as the countryside slid by. She did not want to end her days alone. Perhaps when she decided she had enough money, she should start paying one of those high-class dating agencies or go on a cruise. Suddenly, the idea of a cruise filled her mind, an idea based on old movies where couples stood by the rail in the moonlight. She would get married and send James an invitation and see how he liked that! Damn James, she thought as the bubble of her dream burst.

She went straight to the office in Mircester, took the invitation to James's engagement party and pinned it up on the noticeboard. Mrs. Freedman trotted over and read it. "Don't dare say anything," said Agatha. "Simply write out a reply and I'll sign it. Where's Toni?"

"She's just phoned. She's wrapped up a missing-teenager case and is on her way back in. Oh, here she is now. And there are some photographs on your desk. Phil said you asked for them."

Agatha studied the photographs. There was a clear shot of Trixie leaving the vicarage, and then the photograph had been cropped to show just the head and shoulders.

"Toni," Agatha hailed her. "I've got Trixie's address from the marriage certificate. She used to live in Cheltenham. Get yourself a coffee while I look up the map and find out exactly where we're going."

Toni filled a mug from the coffee machine in the corner of the office. Then she saw the card pinned to the noticeboard. Her first thought was not about how Agatha might be taking the news of her ex's engagement, but about how awkward it would be to see Harry again. Of course, he might not get an invitation. It was not as if he worked for the agency any more.

"Right," said Agatha. "We're off. We'll take my car. Do you mind driving, Toni? I came straight from London and I'm feeling a bit tired."

"Sure," said Toni, reflecting that it was odd of Agatha to let her drive and then wondering for the first time just how badly Agatha was upset by that engagement invitation.

"This could be a wild-goose chase," said Agatha, settling into the passenger seat and fastening her seat belt. "Maybe it's because I really don't like Trixie and I do want it to be her. But what motive could she possibly have?"

"Was that engagement invitation a surprise?" ventured Toni cautiously.

"A bit," said Agatha gruffly.

After a while, Agatha fell asleep. Toni stopped the car and gently removed a smouldering cigarette from Agatha's fingers, stubbed it out in the ashtray and then drove on.

Poor old thing, thought Toni. As she approached Cheltenham, she saw a police car driven by a young woman. It would be nice to work with young people for a change, thought Toni, because Agatha's fifty-something years seemed very old to her.

She nudged Agatha. "Wake up! I need directions."

"Eh, what? I wasn't really asleep," said Agatha defiantly. "Go in on the London Road and then cut up to Montpelier Terrace. Puddleton Close is up the back on the left."

When they reached Montpelier Terrace, Agatha said, "Turn left here and then third on the right and then left again. It's a cul-se-sac. Number four-A, which means it's probably a basement flat. Oh, damn!"

"What?"

"Wait a minute while I phone Patrick. I'll see if one of his old cop friends can check the police records under her name."

Toni waited until Agatha had given Patrick his instructions and then asked, "So do we get out and start to question the neighbours?"

"No, I think I'd like to hear from Patrick first, and I'm hungry. The only food I got on the train was one ghastly little dried-up croissant. We'll leave the car here. There's an antique-gallery place near here with a café."

Agatha ordered a bacon sandwich and coffee in the café. "I wish Patrick would hurry up," she mumbled between bites.

"Might take all day," Toni pointed out. "He's got to find his friend first."

"Well, we'll give it another half an hour."

Toni scowled into her cup of coffee.

"What's bothering you?" asked Agatha. "Half an hour seems like too long?"

"No, I was thinking about sex."

"At your age, that's all anyone thinks about," said Agatha.

"I don't mean it the way you think I mean it. It all frightens me a bit."

"You're a virgin?"

"Yes, still. I got scared off."

Agatha lit a cigarette, saw the horrified look the waitress gave her, remembered the smoking ban and sulkily stubbed it out in her saucer.

"Tell me about it."

"It was in my final year at school," said Toni. "There

was this fellow. All the girls were mad for him and I was flattered when he asked me out on a date. We'd had a bit too much to drink at a club and then he led me down an alley at the back of the club and pushed me up against the wall and began to tear at my clothes. I screamed my head off, pushed him away and ran for my life.

"He put it about the school that I was a frigid lesbian and they all seemed to believe him until he was up in court on a charge of rape. I think I'm too romantic for sex."

"The fact is," said Agatha, "that women's sexual freedom is less than it ever was."

"What about the pill?"

"Oh, that's all right. Saves a lot of unwanted children from being born. But now women are expected to perform all the tricks of the brothel, shave their pubic hair and go in for any nasty deviations the men want. That's not freedom. That's domination. But stick it out, Toni. You're a pretty girl and bright. You'll meet someone nice."

Agatha's phone rang. She scrambled in her handbag for her mobile. "Yes, Patrick," Toni heard her say. Agatha listened intently, a smile spreading across her face. Finally she said, "That's great work. Type it out and leave it on my desk in the office." She rang off.

"Listen to this, Toni. Fifteen years ago, the saintly vicar's wife was booked for possession and for supplying acid at the clubs. Why on earth she married a vicar, I'll never know. Let's go round to Puddleton Close and see what we can dig up."

"It looks very upmarket," said Toni as she parked once more outside 4-A.

"A lot of these places have been gentrified," said Agatha. "Let's see if there's anyone at home."

They walked down the stairs to the basement flat and rang the bell. The door was opened by a slim young man wearing jeans and an open-necked shirt. He had a shock of ginger hair and a pleasant face marred by acne scars.

Agatha explained they were private detectives trying to find out about a certain Trixie Webster who had lived in the flat fifteen years ago.

"No use asking me," he said. "I only moved in a month ago and I think three sets of people lived here before me. Try old Mrs. Brother. She lives in the top flat and she's lived there for yonks."

Agatha thanked him. She and Toni climbed the stairs out of the basement and up to the main front door. Agatha rang the bell marked "Brother." An elderly voice came over the intercom demanding to know who was there.

Agatha patiently explained her business. There was a long silence while she fretted on the doorstep, and then, to her relief, the door was buzzed open.

Mrs. Brother was waiting for them on the landing

at the top of the stairs. She was stooped and wrinkled and seemed very old indeed, but her eyes were bright and sharp.

"Come in," she said.

They entered a low-ceilinged, sunny room. Unlike most homes of the elderly, the room was neither over-furnished nor filled with photographs. There was a good landscape over the fireplace. A sofa and two comfortable chairs were covered in faded chintz facing a low coffee table. A Persian rug lay on the polished boards on the floor. There was a small polished round table with three upright chairs by the window holding a little crystal glass of wild flowers.

"Please sit down," said Mrs. Brother.

Agatha's eyes fell on a large glass ashtray on the coffee table. "Do you smoke, Mrs. Brother?"

"Yes, I enjoy the occasional cigarette."

Agatha pulled out her cigarette packet and offered her one. I can go on smoking if this ancient lady can still smoke and feel no ill effects, thought Agatha.

Mrs. Brother lit up a cigarette and fell into a paroxysm of coughing. "I shouldn't really," she wheezed when she could speak.

Agatha decided not to have a cigarette after all.

"Can you tell me anything about Trixie Webster?"

"I remember her. I was the one who phoned the police. She was squatting with a bunch of hippies in the basement. They played music so loudly that the whole building seemed to vibrate. My husband was alive then and went down to give them a ticking-off. Trixie threw a glass of vodka in his face and I do not wish to repeat what she said to him, but it was mostly four-letter words. When he told me, I called the police. It was hard to get the police to come even in those days, so I lied and said I thought they had guns.

"They raided the place and to my delight, they actually found a gun—a sawn-off shotgun. Mark Murphy—he was married to Trixie at that time—was sent away for a long time because it transpired the shotgun had been used in a bank hold-up. They also found a large quantity of drugs. It was Trixie's first offence and she got off lightly because she testified against the others. After that, I read in the local paper that she had been caught again for supplying drugs at a pop concert."

"Do you know she is now a vicar's wife?"

"What is the name of this vicar?"

"Mr. Arthur Chance. I wonder how she met him?"

"Who knows? Maybe he was prison-visiting. Why are you asking about her? Wait a minute. That fête in Comfrey Magna where there was LSD in the jam?"

Agatha nodded her head.

"And two women dead because of it! Trixie Webster is a wicked woman."

"I wonder why the police didn't get on to her," said Toni.

"I remember she was charged under her married

name of Murphy," said Mrs. Brother. "And I don't think the police would suspect a vicar's wife. What will you do now? Have you any real evidence?"

"No," said Agatha slowly. "But if she testified against one of her former friends and was looking for some acid, they may have heard of it. Can you remember exactly when it was that she was charged with the others?"

"You'll need to wait a minute. I kept a newspaper cutting in my scrapbook."

Mrs. Brother stubbed out her cigarette and got painfully to her feet. She was doubled up with another frightening fit of coughing. Must really give it up, thought Agatha.

She seemed to be gone a long time. The flat was very quiet. "Do you think she's dead?" whispered Toni.

"Don't even think about it," Agatha whispered back. "I should never have let her have that cigarette."

There was at last a shuffling sound and Mrs. Brother came back into the room carrying a heavy scrapbook. Toni leaped to her feet and took it from her. "Put it on the table by the window," said Mrs. Brother.

She opened the book to where she had marked a place with a slip of paper. "There it is."

They had all given the Puddleton Close address except one, a certain Cherry Upfield, whose address was listed as 5, Bybry Close, Cheltenham. Agatha took out her notebook and wrote it down. She turned to Mrs. Brother. "If she was Trixie Murphy when she was living here and I asked you about a Trixie Webster, how did you make the connection?"

Mrs. Brother smiled. "It's obvious, isn't it? The name Trixie and drugs and by the time she was booked for possession, she was booked under the name of Webster. She must have been divorced by then and her picture was in the newspapers. This is all very exciting. Will you come back and see me and let me know what happens?"

Agatha promised but, outside, asked Toni to make a note of it. She did not want to think she might forget her promise.

When they were in the car, Agatha said, "Hand me that map of Cheltenham out of the glove compartment. Let me see, Bybry Close. It's actually in Charlton Kings. Get back out on the London Road and I'll direct you from there."

"Surely it's quicker from here," said Toni.

"Probably. But I've been lost in Charlton Kings so many times, I prefer to go the way that I know I can find my way round the one-way system."

"Such a long time," said Toni. "Fifteen years! She may be long gone."

"Need to just hope," said Agatha, reflecting sadly that, to her, fifteen years ago sometimes felt like yesterday.

Bybry Close had an air of genteel decay. Some of the houses were bravely painted in pastel colours, but most had faded dirty stucco fronts and weedy little gardens full of the detritus of old prams and children's broken toys.

Toni rang the bell. After a few minutes, she said, "I don't think it's working," and knocked loudly at the door.

A woman in her forties answered the door. Toni felt disappointed. Surely this plump little woman with a round rosy face and conservative clothes could not be Cherry Upfield.

But Agatha pushed past Toni and demanded, "Cherry Upfield?"

"Yes. Who wants to know?"

Agatha patiently explained who they were and that she wanted to ask questions about Trixie Webster.

"That cow," said Cherry vindictively. "I hope she's dead somewhere with a needle in her arm."

"Don't you read the newspapers or watch television?" asked Agatha. "She's now a vicar's wife and lives in Comfrey Magna."

"Was that her? Blimey. I thought she looked a bit like the Trixie I used to know, but I thought she couldn't possibly be. She was a redhead when I knew her, although, mind you, she dyed her hair. Come in."

She ushered them into a cluttered living room lined with books. "So what's Trixie got to do with the goings-on at Comfrey Magna?" asked Cherry when they were seated.

"We don't know," said Agatha. Toni was pleased with that "we." Agatha usually said "I," as if Toni were not present. "But we've just found out her drugs background and that she testified against you and the others. If she wanted to get hold of some acid, who would she go to?"

"I don't know. I'm long out of the drugs scene. Then, after she testified against us, no one would want to know her. But someone who was really into selling the stuff was Zak Nulty. I saw him the other day going into that pub, the Blodgers, on the Cirencester Road. You could try him, if you can find him."

"What does he look like?" asked Toni.

"He's very tall and thin and when I spotted him, he hadn't changed all that much except he was going bald at the front and had his hair tied back in a grey ponytail."

"Whereabouts on the Cirencester Road?" asked Agatha.

"Just after the T-junction on the London Road. On the left."

They thanked her and promised to let her know of any outcome.

At the pub, there was no sign of Zak Nulty, but they realized they were hungry and ordered sandwiches and drinks.

The pub began to fill up with an unsavoury-looking crowd of young people. Several of the men were eyeing up Toni. They probably think I'm her mother, thought Agatha dismally.

After an hour, Toni said, "We may have missed him in the crowd. Let's look outside. He may have gone to the bar, got a drink and gone outside for a smoke. There are a few tables outside."

Outside the pub, a large crowd was standing, filling the air with blue smoke. Toni nudged Agatha. Sitting at one of the tables was a tall thin man with a ponytail.

Boldly Agatha walked up to him. "Zak Nulty?"

"Who you?"

"Someone who's willing to pay you for a few minutes of your time—in private."

He grinned and rose to his feet. They followed him to the side of the pub. "Now, what's it about?"

"Trixie Webster."

"Who?"

But his eyes flickered.

Agatha opened her handbag and took out a roll of notes which she always carried tucked away in case she needed to bribe someone.

He looked at the notes and said slowly, "What if I do?"

"Did she ask you for any LSD recently? We're not the police."

"I'll put it this way," said Zak slowly. "You tell the police and I'll find you and break your legs."

"Okay," said Agatha. "I just want to know."

"You someone from that village where she lives?"

"Yes," lied Agatha.

He eyed the notes greedily. "How much is there?"

"Five hundred."

He hesitated and then said, "Well, I don't owe that bitch nothing. Yes, I got her some acid. Now, give me the money and don't let me see you again and if the pigs come for me, you're toast."

Agatha handed over the money and she and Toni hurried off to the car park.

Toni drove off a little way and then parked the car. "Now, what do we do?" she asked.

"Tell Bill."

"What! No confronting the suspect like Poirot? And what if Zak comes looking for us?"

"Let me think. I know. We now know for sure that Zak is dealing drugs. We tell Bill to get the police to pick him up for dealing and possession. Then they can cut a deal with him. He testifies he gave Trixie the acid and that's that. Let's get to police headquarters."

But they were told that Bill was at home. Agatha's heart sank. Bill's parents always surveyed her as if something particularly nasty had turned up on their doorstep.

Cherry Upfield fed her cat and settled down in front of her television set to watch a late edition of *Midlands News*. She sat up straight as a shot of a church covered in scaffolding came into view and the presenter said,

"Repairs have begun on the church in Comfrey Magna, scene of recent extraordinary events." As Cherry watched, there was an interview with the vicar, and standing next to him, smiling sweetly, was Trixie.

Cherry's eyes narrowed. That smug bitch. She'd still like to get even with her. She lifted the receiver on the phone next to her chair and dialled directory inquiries and asked for the number of Arthur Chance at the vicarage in Comfrey Magna.

The phone rang several times and then a woman answered.

"Trixie?" asked Cherry.

"Yes, who is this?"

Got a posh voice now, thought Cherry. "It's me, Cherry Upfield."

"I'm afraid I don't know you," said Trixie firmly, and Cherry was suddenly sure she was about to hang up.

"Wait! I just want to give you a warning. Do you know Agatha Raisin?"

"Go on."

"She's on your trail. Got your drugs background. I hope you didn't get any acid from Zak because that was where she was heading when I left."

Trixie hung up and stood, breathing hard. "Who was it?" called Arthur.

"A well-wisher," said Trixie.

———

Agatha and Toni, having passed the formidable barrier that was Mrs. Wong who had grumbled at the lateness of the hour, told Bill all they had found out.

He listened to them with excitement. "We never thought of checking a vicar's wife out," he said. "We'll get on to it in the morning."

"Be sure you get Zak before he gets us," said Agatha. "He said he would break my legs if I told the police."

"Leave it with me."

"So that's that," said Agatha as she said goodnight to Toni after dropping her off at her flat. "Thanks for all the driving. I'm still so tired, I'll be glad to get home."

Once in her cottage, Agatha unwound the cats from around her ankles and decided to check her answering service.

There was one message from Mrs. Bloxby. She said, "I hope it's all right. I gave Mrs. Chance your address. She said she had some news that might help you."

Agatha checked that the burglar alarm was on. She wondered whether to phone Bill and then decided to do it in the morning.

She slept uneasily, wishing not for the first time that she had bought a modern house and not an old thatched cottage where the timbers creaked and the thatch rustled.

In the morning she showered and dressed and went downstairs. She opened her front door to bring in the pint of milk that she had ordered to be delivered every day. Agatha drank her coffee black but liked to have milk in the fridge for her pampered cats and for any visitors. She wondered where Charles was and wished he would leave a note every time he went away to say when he would be back. She debated whether to phone him but did not feel like dealing with his man, Gustav, who delighted in telling her that Charles was not at home, even when he was.

She was bending down to pick up the bottle of milk when she saw a little dead bird lying beside it. Blue tits had a habit of pecking through the foil top of the milk and drinking the cream. Agatha went back into her cottage on shaking legs and called the police.

Bill and Wilkes turned up, followed by a forensic team. Agatha explained how Mrs. Bloxby had left her a message to say that Trixie had called, asking for her address. The little bird was bagged up and the milk bottle sealed and taken away.

Agatha suddenly had a horrible idea. "The office!" she exclaimed. "There's milk delivered there. I'd better phone Toni and tell her to get round there and make sure no one touches it. Nobody's due at the office for another hour."

"We'll send a policewoman round there to meet her," said Wilkes.

Toni hurried round to the office. She looked down at the bottle of milk outside and decided it would be best to leave it until the police arrived. She unlocked the door and went in.

She was just jacking up her computer when she heard a knock at the door. "Come in," she called over her shoulder.

Toni heard someone come in. "Did you get the milk?" she asked.

"No, but you're going to get it."

Toni swung round and stared in alarm at Trixie Chance, who was standing there with a knife in one hand and the bottle of milk in the other.

"You and that lesbian boss of yours have ruined my life," said Trixie. "Let's see what she feels when she finds her little creature dead on the office floor—although she's probably dead herself by now."

"I'm not a lesbian and neither is Agatha," said Toni, standing up. "Put down the knife."

Toni moved behind her typing chair.

"Why couldn't you leave me alone?" snarled Trixie.

"Because you caused the deaths of two women," said Toni, while inside her head her mind raced. To have survived a brutal childhood, to have come out of it all into the sunshine of a glorious life and to have it threatened by this madwoman. Toni felt herself beginning to burn up with white-hot rage. She grasped the back of her wheeled typing chair and ran with it, slamming it into Trixie and sending her flying just as the door opened and a policewoman and policeman rushed in. Trixie was making a dive for the knife, which had fallen out of her hand, when the policewoman fired her Taser gun into her back.

The policeman handcuffed Trixie while the policewoman said, "She'll come round any minute now. What happened here?"

Toni told her about Agatha's warning. The police called for forensics and told headquarters to tell Wilkes of the latest development.

More police arrived. Toni repeated her story over and over again while a recovered Trixie was taken away, swearing horribly.

By the time Toni arrived at police headquarters to make an official statement, the press were gathered outside.

Inside, she was relieved to find that she was to be questioned by Bill and Wilkes. She had dreaded being interviewed by the bullying Collins.

When the interview was over, Bill said, "Do you want us to call your mother?"

"No, it's all right," said Toni. "She's living in Southampton now. I'll be fine."

"You'll find Agatha waiting for you."

Still suffering from shock, Toni went out into reception to find Agatha sitting there. She eyed her uneasily. What if Agatha was a lesbian and that was the reason for all her generosity?

"Why are you looking at me like that?" demanded Agatha. "Have I got a smut on my nose?"

"Trixie said you were a lesbian," Ton blurted out.

Agatha began to laugh. When she had finished laughing, she said, "Sometimes I wish I were. It would make life a lot easier. Men! I phoned Charles for support and he answered his phone for once and said he couldn't make it because he had some female staying with him. Now, tell me what went on."

Toni sat down next to her and wearily described again what had happened.

"Well, if the forensics turn up trumps, they've got her for two counts of attempted murder," said Agatha, "so that's good enough to be going on with. I've still to make an official statement, so I'll be here for a while. Why don't you take the rest of the day off? I've told the others to do the same. Forensics will be working in the office for most of the day."

Toni emerged and blinked as a battery of flashes went off in her face. The chief constable, George Robinson, was addressing the press. He put an arm around Toni's slim shoulders. "All I can tell you," he said, "is that this brave private detective tackled someone who was attempting to murder her. I will make a further statement later."

Agatha heard the commotion and opened the door. "This way, Toni!" the photographers were shouting.

I'm the boss, thought Agatha jealously. It should be *my* press conference.

But as she was about to push forward, Wilkes tapped

her on the shoulder. "We're ready for you now, Mrs. Raisin."

Agatha sat gloomily over the newspapers the next morning, reflecting sourly that Toni photographed like a dream with the sunlight glinting on her fair hair and her wide blue eyes and slim figure.

She switched on the television. There was a late bulletin to say that Trixie Chance, wife of the vicar of Saint Odo The Severe, had been charged with two counts of manslaughter and two counts of attempted murder and with possession of an illegal substance.

Agatha began to resent Toni. That girl kept getting all the glory. She wondered whether it might be an idea to set Toni up in her own agency. Then let's see how she fared without the genius of Agatha Raisin to help her. Her own agency was doing well. She could certainly afford to fund Toni until the girl got on her feet, and if she didn't, she could write it off as a tax loss.

Fired up with this new idea, Agatha phoned Toni and told her to make herself free for a business lunch at one o'clock in the George, a pub opposite police headquarters

Toni expected Agatha to be sour over the press coverage and was relieved to see a beaming Agatha waiting for her in the restaurant. Agatha had not been in the office that morning.

"Sit down," said Agatha. "We'll order our food and drinks first. The steak and kidney pudding here is very good and I feel like some comfort food."

"I'm sorry about taking the limelight in the press coverage," said Toni.

Agatha waved a dismissive hand. "It's all good for the agency. I have a plan for you."

"Like what?" asked Toni nervously.

"Wait till we get our food. What are you drinking?"

"Mineral water will do fine," said Toni, "and the steak and kidney pudding."

When Agatha returned from the bar after placing their order, Toni said, "Why did she do it?"

"Who? What?"

"Trixie. I mean, she had a respectable life. Why did she put acid in the jam?"

"Because she's mad."

"Even mad people have a reason."

Agatha took out her phone and called Patrick. "Patrick," she said, "did any of your police contacts give you any reason why Trixie did what she did?"

Toni could hear the tinny sound of Patrick's reply but not the words.

"Well, I'll be damned!" exclaimed Agatha. "See you later."

She turned to Toni. "You're not going to believe this. Evidently Trixie said she did it because she was bored and wanted to liven the village up a bit."

"Awful woman," said Toni with a shudder. "Mind you, if she hadn't come after us, she might just have got away with it."

Their food arrived. Toni waited impatiently until Agatha had taken a few mouthfuls of food and then asked, "What's this idea?"

"I'm going to set you up in your own detective agency," said Agatha.

"But I don't know how to run a business!"

"You'll learn. You're bright. Employ a secretary and two young people like yourself. No old detectives. We'll call it the Spring Detective Agency. You know— spring—youth."

"What about the Gilmour Detective Agency?"

"No, I don't think so. Start thinking about who you would recruit and I'll look around for premises."

Toni knew in that moment that Agatha resented the press coverage she had got. She reflected that it's a sad business to find out the rock you've been leaning on for support has a great crack down the middle.

"Think about it," said Agatha, feeling obscurely ashamed of herself. "If you don't want to do it, don't bother."

Toni was pretty sure that she would turn down Agatha's offer. But something was to happen which changed her mind.

Chapter Eleven

Toni was sitting that evening with her friend Sharon when the phone rang. It was Harry.

"I just wondered how you were getting on," he said.

"I'm fine," said Toni, and then, in a rush, she went on, "I'm not really. Agatha wants to set me up in my own detective agency and I don't think I can do it. I don't know anything about running a business."

"I wonder why she's doing that," said Harry. "I tell you what, I'll take a year off from university and help you set up. I'm bored with Cambridge and I miss the detective work."

"No ties?" asked Toni anxiously.

"No, no. Strictly business. It would be exciting."

Toni felt a wave of relief. "If you're free, drop round and we'll talk about it."

"Be with you in minutes."

"Who was that?" asked Sharon.

"Harry."

"Not the fellow who wants you to read them Frenchies and go to crap opera?"

"Yes, but he says it's strictly business and I do need the help. He's coming round."

"Great. I'm dying to see what this wannabe professor looks like."

Harry arrived so quickly that Toni wondered if he had been lurking at the corner of her street.

Sharon eyed him with surprise. Harry, who had once worn a nose stud and shaved his head, now had a crop of wavy brown hair above a square handsome face. He was dressed smart-casual. Toni introduced them.

"Let's get started," said Harry. "Is Agatha hiring the staff for you?"

"No, she wants me to hire young people."

"Does she want you to fail?" asked Harry. "I mean, a retired copper like Patrick is a boon."

"Why would she want me to fail?"

"Well, not fail. I've seen you on television. You have been taking the limelight away from her."

"I don't like the sound of this," said Toni.

"Oh, go for it. What about a name?"

"She wants me to call it Spring, as in youth."

"We can't have that. What about Gilmour Detective Agency?"

"I suggested that and she turned it down."

"She *is* jealous. Let me think."

"Why not just call it The Detective Agency?" said Sharon.

"Oh, I like that," said Harry. "She'll go for it because it sounds modest at first. When we get set up, we'll put the *The* in italics. Now, we need a secretary."

"I could do that," said Sharon. "I'm good on computers."

"You've got the job," said Toni quickly because Harry was looking doubtfully at the appearance Sharon made that evening. She had dyed her masses of hair blonde with aubergine streaks, and her plump figure was encased in tight jeans torn at the knee and a pink sequinned crop top showing a bulge of fake-tanned midriff.

"What about Betty Talent?" asked Sharon. "You know, Miss Iron Knickers, the school swot. Ever so clever she was."

"She's probably at university," said Toni.

"No, she went abroad for a gap year and got some sort of tropical bug. She's been recovering. I've got her number."

"Why? You were always jeering at her," said Toni.

"When I heard she was ill, I felt sorry for her," said Sharon. "I was sure nobody would go to see her, so I took her a box of chocolates. She's pretty nice when you get to know her."

"Everyone, including me, will need to be on trial," said Harry. "You'd better warn her. She may not want the job."

"I'll phone her." Sharon retreated to a corner of the room.

"Look," said Toni. "Agatha's paying for all this, so she'll probably want a say in what we call the agency."

"I'll fund it," said Harry. "An uncle of mine died recently and left me a lot of money. You make it pay and I'll get my money back."

Charles, who had turned up unexpectedly, was sitting at the moment with Agatha in the village pub, the Red Lion, listening as Agatha tried to justify setting Toni up in her own detective agency.

He waited until she had finished and then said carefully, "You're hoping it'll keep her out of the limelight."

"How dare you! I'm not petty."

"Just jealous."

"Well, if this is going to be the general reaction," said Agatha huffily, "I'll cancel the whole idea." Agatha reflected that the only person these days who seemed to be pleased with her was old Mrs. Brother, whom she had phoned earlier to give her a full report of the arrest of Trixie. Her phone rang. "Yes, Toni," Charles heard her say and then watched with amusement the growing dismay on Agatha's face. Then he heard her say, "And you're going to do the whole thing yourself? Find premises? If I'm going to pay for this, I should at least have a say . . . What? Harry is going to fund it? My Harry?

Harry Beam? Oh, well, if that's the way you feel. Good luck."

She rang off and stared at the table, looking moodily at the cigarette burns and remembering the glory days when she could light a cigarette.

"So Harry Beam is going to run the show?" asked Charles.

"Yes, it's a good idea," said Agatha, struggling to be fair. "I'm sure they'll make a go of it."

"You know, Aggie, if she'd been a failure, you'd have hated yourself. Let it go. What ever happened to that drug pusher, Zak somebody?"

"The police got him."

"I heard he got out on bail."

"Oh, God. He said he would break my legs."

Betty Talent seemed a quiet, dowdy girl. She had no-colour hair scraped back from a small neat face. She was very thin. Her one beauty was her eyes, which were very large and brown flecked with green. She was wearing a long jacket over a straight skirt, a white blouse buttoned up to the neck, and flat shoes.

But when it came to costing what they would need to set up the business, Betty turned out to be a genius. As she crunched the numbers, her eyes began to glow with enthusiasm.

"This is great," said Harry. "When we get some

money in, we'll start to buy surveillance equipment. I think we should start off with just us—that's Toni Gilmour as boss, me, Harry Beam, Sharon . . . ?"

"Gold."

"Sharon Gold and Betty Talent."

"I've got a bottle of champagne a local newspaper gave me," said Toni. "Let's drink a toast to *The* Detective Agency."

When she came back with the bottle and glasses, Betty said, "You said you would fund this, Harry. Will you have to get the money from your father?"

"No, an uncle of mine died and left me a lot. No worries."

On the Saturday morning Agatha received a visit from Mrs. Bloxby. "I wondered if you would like to come with me to Comfrey Magna," said Mrs. Bloxby. "I feel poor Mr. Chance could do with some consolation."

"He'll hate me," said Agatha. "I'm the one who got his wife banged up."

"I think it would help if you could explain to him what actually happened. If he still believes his wife innocent, he could be in great pain."

Curiosity got the better of Agatha. "Right, I'll go."

There was a faint mist curling around the boles of the trees and coloured leaves sailed lazily down onto the road. As she drove the now-familiar road to Comfrey

Magna, Agatha wondered what to wear for James's engagement party. Then she thought of hair extensions. Trixie had looked good with them. But not blonde, thought Agatha. I tried blonde once and it didn't work. I wonder what his fiancée looks like. Please, God, let her look like a bag.

Agatha parked in front of the church. As they walked across the graveyard, she remembered the first time she had seen George. What a terrible mistake it had been to fall for good looks. "I'm sorry I wasn't much help to you in finding out about Mrs. Chance's background," said Mrs. Bloxby, "but I did try."

"Doesn't matter now," said Agatha. "I wonder if George is still around."

"No. That bit of news I did hear. He married Miss Corrie and they have gone to Cornwall on their honeymoon."

"Good luck to her." Agatha rang the bell.

To her surprise, the door was answered by Phyllis Tolling. "Oh, it's you," she said. "What do you want?"

"We have called to see Mr. Chance."

"It's hardly a good time. The poor man is still in shock."

Then Agatha heard Arthur's voice raised in song.

"When he thinks that he is past love,
That is when he meets his last love,
And he loves her like he never loved before."

A smile crossed Phyllis's face. "Come in," she said.

Arthur was in the living room, surrounded by packing cases. "Hullo!" he hailed them. "Just packing away Trixie's things. I don't think she'll be needing them for a long time. Tea?"

"That would be nice," said Mrs. Bloxby.

"I'll get it, darling," said Phyllis.

"Oh, you are good." Arthur blew her a kiss.

Agatha decided that Arthur did not need any consoling words, so instead she asked, "I often wondered how you met Trixie."

"It was just after my second wife died," said the vicar.

Mrs. Bloxby looked at him nervously. "What did your wives die of?"

Arthur roared with laughter. "Frightened I bumped them off? No, Jane, the first had cancer and Cressida, the second, had a stroke, poor thing. I was holidaying in Brighton and I met Trixie by chance in the hotel lounge. She told me she was just divorced and began to cry. One thing led to another and we got married. Oh, tea. Splendid, splendid."

"I'll be through in the bedroom," said Phyllis, putting down the tray. "I'll go on packing up the clothes."

"Good girl. What would I do without you?"

While they drank their tea, Mrs. Bloxby gently turned the conversation to general parish matters until they got up to leave.

"What did you think of that?" asked Agatha eagerly as they drove off.

"I think that Mr. Chance is a very *lustful* man."

"A what?"

"Yes, one cannot always go by appearances."

After Agatha had dropped Mrs. Bloxby off at the vicarage and had gone to her cottage, she found she was plagued with uneasiness.

She began to dread the thought of announcing to the others that Toni was going to start her own agency. They would think she was a jealous, petty woman.

"I think I am," said Agatha gloomily to her cats. She phoned Toni. "Perhaps this new agency business is not such a good idea," said Agatha. "Perhaps you should work for me for a few more years and—"

"But it's a brilliant idea," cried Toni. "We'll be ready to start in several weeks."

"What about Harry? Are you sure he doesn't have an ulterior motive?"

"Oh, no. He's as excited as I am. I don't know how to thank you. If it's as successful as I hope it will be, I can pay you back all the money you spent on me."

"That won't be necessary," said Agatha. "Good luck."

She rang off and glared balefully at her cats. "Just thank your stars I'm not a cat-kicking person."

There was a ring at the doorbell. Agatha rushed to answer it and found Bill Wong on the doorstep.

"Come in," she cried. "I've got some coffee ready."

"I had a phone call from Toni," said Bill and Agatha's heart sank. "She told me all about this new-agency idea, said it was your idea. Why did you want to get rid of your best detective?"

"I felt I was holding her back," Agatha lied.

"You felt she was stealing your thunder," said Bill.

"That's not the reason!"

"Let's talk about something else. Zak is out on bail."

"So I heard."

"Well, he promised to testify against Trixie and bail was part of the deal. Then she confessed, but it was too late to reverse it. Don't worry. He's in deep enough trouble without coming after you. Anything else happening?"

Agatha told him about Arthur Chance. "He'll probably marry Phyllis," she said.

"He's old, he's wrinkled, he's got grey hair and thick glasses. Why do people like that get all the luck when you and I are stuck with singlehood, Agatha?"

"Think about it, Bill. Would you have married Trixie or given Phyllis a second look?"

He grinned. "Not really. Doing anything today?"

"No."

"Feel like a trip to Bramley Park?"

"What! The place with the swings and roundabouts and the roller coaster?"

"That's the place. Come on. I've never been on a roller coaster."

Agatha enjoyed herself immensely and screamed for the whole length of the roller coaster ride.

She drove home in the evening feeling tired and happy.

Agatha checked her answering service. There was one message from Cherry Upfield. She said, "I've got some more information on Trixie if you need it. I'll be home all evening."

Agatha phoned her to say that she would call on her in the morning but got no reply. She then called Toni. Sharon answered the phone. "She's not here," she said. "We were out all day and then she got a phone call from some woman saying she had more information on Trixie, so she's just shot off."

Why both of us? wondered Agatha, slowly replacing the phone. Agatha then phoned Bill on his mobile, praying he would answer. Mrs. Wong disapproved of his using his mobile in the house and he usually had it switched off. To her relief he answered and she quickly told him about the message. "I don't like it," said Agatha. "I think it might have something to do with Zak."

"Then stay there," ordered Bill. "I'll get some men and go over."

But Agatha couldn't rest. She felt sure Toni was in danger. She rushed to her car and set off, driving at furious speed towards Cheltenham.

She parked at the end of the close and cautiously made her way on foot. She walked past Cherry's house. The lights were on, but the curtains were drawn. Agatha walked to the other end of the close and found a lane leading round to the back.

She looked back and counted the number of houses and then entered the lane, counting her way along until she was sure she was at the back of Cherry's house.

She tried the garden gate and found it was open. She took a small pencil torch out of her handbag and made her way cautiously up to the back of the house.

I wish I had a gun, she thought. Where are the police?

She tried the handle of the kitchen door. It wasn't locked. She eased her way in, flicking her torch this way and that, looking for a weapon.

The beam of the torch fell on an overflowing litterbin. Agatha looked around the shelves and took down a bottle of cooking oil and poured it over the contents of the bin. Then she took out her lighter and lit the top of the rubbish.

With the bottle of oil in her hand, she stood behind the kitchen door. The rubbish went up with a roar. "Hurry up," muttered Agatha. "I'm going to be fried to a crisp."

She eased the kitchen door open so that the flames could be seen from the living room. She heard a curse and Zak erupted into the kitchen. He opened the back door and kicked the flaming bin of rubbish into the garden. He stood with his hands on his hips and was about to turn around when Agatha struck him on the head with the bottle of oil. He sank to his knees, but he was not unconscious. Terrified, Agatha began to throw everything she could get off the shelves straight at him just as she heard the police come bursting into the house.

"In here!" screamed Agatha, hurling a container of drinking chocolate at Zak, followed by half a dozen eggs.

The police, headed by Bill, charged into the kitchen. Zak was handcuffed and dragged upright, egg and cocoa and other foodstuffs dripping off him.

"Toni!" cried Agatha, pushing her way into the living room.

A policeman was releasing Toni and Cherry, who had been tied to two upright chairs and gagged.

Toni got shakily to her feet. Agatha hugged her and said, "Oh, I couldn't bear to lose you."

Toni gave her a watery smile and said, "I didn't know you cared," and burst into tears.

It was to be a long night. Agatha was strongly reprimanded for not staying out of it. Toni protested, saying Zak had threatened that as soon as Agatha arrived he was going to break both their legs and flee the country. She said that she was sure when he heard the police arriving, he would have broken *her* legs and fled out the back way. Cherry said she had been forced at knifepoint into making the phone calls before she, too, had been tied up.

The press had got wind of a story and were waiting outside the police station. Toni, although warned by Collins not to say a word, made a statement saying her life had been saved by the best detective in the world, Agatha Raisin, but that she could not say any more until the trial.

Well, that's that, thought Agatha as she wearily drove home. Life goes on. All the loose ends tied up except for the death of George's wife. I'll probably never know now.

Fred and George Selby were celebrating their honeymoon in a picturesque hotel high on the cliffs near the Cornish village of Tryvithek. George had gone down to the bar for a drink, where Fred was to join him when she was ready.

She was just collecting her handbag when she noticed George had left his mobile phone. Curiosity overcame her. She wondered if he had any text messages. She clicked them on. She stared down at the first one in horror. It read, "Will you really have the money soon, my darling? Can't wait. Love, Gilda."

Fred sank slowly down onto the bed. Her knees were

trembling. She remembered the article about Gilda. She remembered all the awful rumours about the death of George's last wife. She thought about the wills they had made out and how they had insured each other's lives. She began to burn up with a furious rage.

"Hullo, darling," said George as Fred walked into the bar. "You look a bit pale. Are you all right?"

"I'm fine. Ready for our walk?"

"Don't you go near the cliffs tonight," warned the barman. "It's blowing up something rough and it's all dark out there."

"We'll be fine," said George, taking Fred's arm. "We'll probably walk down to the village."

If he goes to the village, thought Fred, I might begin to think I imagined that message. He *must* love me!

But George said, "Look there's a moon. And I do like to walk the cliffs and see the giant waves pounding at the foot of them."

"Let go of my arm," said Fred. "I want to swing my arms as I walk. It's a bit cold. Let's go back in."

"Just a bit further," said George. He walked to the cliff's edge, his thick fair hair blowing in the wind. "Come and look at this. The waves are enormous."

Fred felt a numb, blank misery. Like a sleepwalker she advanced on her husband, who was peering over the edge. With all her strength, she gave him one almighty push. The tussocky grass under his feet was slippery with recent rain. He skidded right over the edge, his cry of despair being lost in the roar of the waves and the screech of the wind as he plunged downwards.

Fred sat down on the wet grass behind a large outcrop of rock and opened her handbag. She took out a packet of skunk, and sheltering it from the wind by opening her coat, she rolled a joint and lit it. She breathed the smoke deep into her lungs.

She smoked on until the whole episode began to seem like a bad dream. Poor silly George, she thought. Gone forever. I'll give him a nice funeral if they ever find the body.

She peered round the rock and let out a scream. A head and shoulders were appearing above the cliff. George had fallen onto a ledge below. He was bruised, battered, frightened and furious.

Fred ran forward and began to kick at his face. He grabbed one of her ankles. She stamped down ferociously on his other hand. He lost his grip and plunged backwards, taking her with him. Still struggling and cursing, they spiralled down and disappeared beneath the boiling sea.

A day later, Agatha answered her door early in the morning to find Mrs. Bloxby on her doorstep. "Have you seen the news this morning?" cried Mrs. Bloxby.

"No, I'm just up. Come in and tell me about it."

"It's about Mr. Selby," said Mrs. Bloxby.

"Gorgeous George. What about him?"

"He's dead!"

"How?"

"A local at that place in Cornwall where they were on honeymoon was walking his dog along the cliffs when he heard cries and shone his torch. He saw a man hanging onto the cliff edge for dear life while a woman was stamping on his fingers. He said the man had the woman by the ankle. He ran forward, but they both plunged into the sea. The coastguard are out looking for the bodies. The witness said it looked as if the man had already been over the cliff and was trying to get back up. What do you think of that?"

Agatha sat down at the kitchen table and lit a cigarette. "It looks as if Fred got wised up to him some way. It really looks now as if George might have wound up poor Sybilla to kill his wife. Maybe Fred knew about it and tried to get him first. I never liked that girl, but now I'm heartily sorry for her, and I hope somewhere up in heaven the first Mrs. Selby is having a good laugh."

"That's sacrilegious, Mrs. Raisin."

"That's human, Mrs. Bloxby."

Epilogue

AGATHA RAISIN SAT HUNCHED up in a first-class railway carriage as the London-to-Mircester train ploughed on through the fog. Why couldn't this be the night when the trains were cancelled? she thought. I don't want to go.

She was heading for James's engagement party after a rigorous makeover in London. Her hair extensions fell to her shoulders in soft waves. Her face was cleverly made up by an expensive beautician. She had been dieting ferociously and the highly expensive midnight-blue silk dress she had spent a fortune on was extremely flattering.

The train, which was often late, perversely drew into the Gothic splendour of Mircester Station exactly two minutes early.

Agatha longed to forget about the whole thing and go home, go to bed and cuddle up to her cats. But everyone would feel sorry for her and she couldn't bear that. Toni had said their new premises would be opening with a party in a week's time. Agatha didn't want to go to that either.

Agatha took a cab to the George, changing on the short journey out of a pair of flat shoes into a pair of high-heeled sandals.

"Here we go," she muttered. "Rehearsal's over. On-stage at last."

A couple leaving the George gave her a nervous look.

She glanced at the noticeboard in the foyer. "Engagement Party—Betjeman Suite."

The Betjeman Suite was so called because the famous poet and lover of Victoriana would have adored it. From its faux medieval ceiling to the enormous marble fireplace at one end, it had not been changed since the hotel was built in 1875.

Agatha left her red cashmere cloak in the cloakroom outside the suite, took a deep breath and made her entrance. She was surrounded by familiar faces and cries of "Agatha, you look fabulous!"

Nervously her eyes scanned the room. Charles came to join her. "Where's James?" asked Agatha.

"He'll be here shortly. They got held up by the fog. Have a drink." Charles grabbed a glass of champagne from a passing waitress and handed it to her.

Agatha looked round. Toni was wearing a skimpy black dress with thin shoulder straps. Her fair hair was piled up on her head and shone under the lights from the huge crystal chandelier above her. I've lost a good detective, thought Agatha bitterly. I've always prided myself on being a good businesswoman and not letting personal feelings get in the way. What went wrong? And so ran Agatha's troubled thoughts, unaware that her whole life had been propelled by emotion.

A cheer went up and Agatha slowly turned round. James stood beaming in the doorway, Felicity Bross-Tilkington on his arm.

Agatha felt any confidence she had left seeping out through the soles of her shoes. Felicity was exquisite. She had wide-spaced grey eyes in a tanned face. Her thick brown hair cascaded down on her shoulders in an artful arrangement of waves and curls. Straight hair, as Agatha knew, had just been damned as passé. Her figure was slim and showed no signs of rigorous dieting. She was wearing a low-cut gold evening top which showed off the smooth perfection of her genuine tan and the stunning necklace of old gold and rubies around her neck.

James looked as proud as Punch as he gazed down at his fiancée. He never once looked at me like that, thought Agatha, but let's face it, I never once looked like that. James led Felicity straight up to Agatha and introduced her. "I am so pleased to meet you," said Felicity. "Goodness, after all James told me about you, I expected to meet someone quite ferocious."

"Here, have another glass of champagne," said Charles at Agatha's side. James introduced him to Felicity. "Come and talk to me, Felicity," said Charles. "I think we know some of the same people."

James smiled at Agatha. "You look great. Long hair suits you. So what do you think of Felicity?"

"She is certainly very beautiful," said Agatha. "Where did you meet?"

"In Paris, at my friend Sylvan's party. Is he here?" He looked around the room. "He's probably held up by the fog. So I have your blessing?" asked James, studying Agatha intently.

"Yes, James."

"You don't think I'm too old for her? She's only thirty-two."

"Doesn't matter for a man. Has she been married before?"

"No."

That's odd, thought Agatha. How does anyone that beautiful get to thirty-two without being married?

Others began to cluster round. Agatha saw Mrs. Bloxby and went over to her. "How do you feel, Mrs. Raisin?" asked Mrs. Bloxby.

Agatha looked at her friend in dawning relief. "Do you know, I feel just fine. I really do. Now that I'm here and I've met her, it's all rather pleasant. James seems like a different person to me now. For the first time in my life, I'm over men."

They were joined by Bill Wong and the staff of the agency and they all began to talk shop.

Mrs. Bloxby joined her husband, who was standing moodily in a corner of the room.

"Can we go now?" he asked.

"Now, really, Alf. We can hardly go now. The party's just begun."

Agatha was aware of James standing beside her and turned round. "Do you *really* wish me well?" he asked.

"Of course. Were you hoping I would be jealous?"

"Something like that."

"But you are in love?"

"Oh, yes. She listens to everything I say and takes an interest in my work, particularly military history. Instead of the travel books, I might suggest doing a series of guides to famous battlefields."

"I always listened to you," said Agatha defiantly.

"I remember one occasion talking to you about the Crimean War and your eyes glazed over."

"I listened to every word!"

"When was it?"

"Can't remember. I never was good at dates. Was that the one with the longbows?"

"That was Agincourt. See? You haven't a clue."

"James, darling. You're neglecting your other guests." Felicity took his arm.

"So I am. Talk to you later, Agatha."

"Wait a bit. When are you getting married?"

"Next April," said James. "Coming to see me off, Agatha?"

"I wouldn't miss it. Where is it to be held?"

"In Downboys in Sussex at the local church."

"I'll be there."

Agatha watched them uneasily as they moved about the room. Why did he hope I would be jealous? wondered Agatha. If I were really in love with someone, for example, it wouldn't even cross my mind to make James jealous.

Roy Silver arrived. He was wearing a dark blue silk shirt and dark blue trousers.

"You look as if you're ready for bed," commented Agatha.

"It shows what you know. This is the latest thing. You've become very provincial, Aggie. Though I must say, you've never looked better. Hair extensions?"

"Yes."

"I hope you didn't get them done cheap. A friend of mine went to a Mr. Bert and he said bits started to fall off in no time at all."

Agatha, who had gone to Mr. Bert, decided to change the subject.

"That's the fiancée over there."

"She's very beautiful. Except for the mouth."

"What's up with her mouth?"

"Too thin and something reptilian about it. Now who is that who's just arrived?"

Agatha looked across to the doorway. Sylvan had arrived. He could not possibly be anything other than

French. He had a beaky nose, a thatch of fair hair streaked with grey, hooded eyes, a mobile mouth and expressive long thin fingers. As James rushed to meet him, Agatha noticed that all Sylvan's expressive gestures were Gallic. He had a tall slim figure with broad shoulders and tiny hips.

A little glow started in Agatha's stomach. A minute before she saw Sylvan, she was aware of her feet beginning to hurt. Now she did not notice the discomfort. Everyone else at the party seemed to fade. In her dazzled mind, Sylvan seemed to be illuminated by a spotlight.

James led Sylvan forward. "Agatha, may I introduce Sylvan Dubois? Sylvan, Agatha Raisin."

"Aha. Your first wife." Sylvan took Agatha's hand. "How on earth did he let you get away?"

Agatha smiled. "James is about to have a very beautiful young second wife."

"Pah! Me, I find the mature woman infinitely attractive."

His grey eyes were flirtatious as he looked down at her.

"Do you live in Paris?"

"Yes, I do."

"And what do you do for a living?"

"Nothing much. My father had a factory for manufacturing bottles. He left it to me when he died. I have an excellent manager, so I have quite a lot of free time."

His English was excellent but spoken with an

attractive French accent. "So what do you do with your free time?"

"Let me see. I get up in the morning, have breakfast, wash and dress and go out to meet friends at the local brasserie. We put the world to rights. Then I have a late lunch and go back to my apartment, where I read and then get changed again and go to the theatre or a cinema."

"And what about Mrs. Dubois?"

"Alas, there isn't one."

"Was there one?"

"A long time ago."

"And what happened?"

He looked amused. "So many questions. But you are a detective, so I suppose it comes naturally to you. Now I have—how do you say—a predicament. A bit of your hair has just floated into my glass of champagne. Do I mention it?"

"You just have," said Agatha, turning fiery red.

He eased it out with one long finger and dropped it on the floor. "You should have got your extensions done in Paris. Don't look so upset. The effect is still dazzling. Do you think James will want to marry you again?"

That distracted Agatha from worrying about her hair. "Why?" she asked in amazement.

"My friend James is an intelligent man and little Felicity is oh, so boring. At the moment, he can only see her appearance. He needs someone like you."

Agatha wanted to say, "And *I* need someone like *you*," but said instead, "Are you here for long?"

"I am driving back to Paris tonight. I only came for this. I shall see you at the wedding."

James and Felicity joined them. "Come and meet some of the others, Sylvan," said Felicity, hooking her arm in his and leading him away.

"Do be careful, Agatha," whispered James.

"What about?"

"Sylvan has the reputation of being a ladykiller."

"Then he can kill me anytime," said Agatha.

"Now you're being silly."

"Don't call me silly. You always used to run me down."

"No, I did not. You love playing the victim, Agatha."

"I am not a victim," howled Agatha.

There was a sudden silence in the room. Then everyone started chattering loudly again.

Agatha stomped off to join the comforting presence of her friend, Mrs. Bloxby. "Where's your husband?" asked Agatha.

"He had a headache and left," said Mrs. Bloxby. "What upset James?"

"He was warning me against Sylvan."

"But he need not worry. You're over bothering about men, aren't you?" asked Mrs. Bloxby anxiously.

"Oh, sure," said Agatha.

Agatha looked across the room and her eyes fastened

on Sylvan talking to a radiant Toni. Her eyes narrowed. "Excuse me," she said.

Mrs. Bloxby watched as her friend deftly cut out Toni and led Sylvan away, watched as she laughed and talked and tossed her hair, unaware of the fact that bits of her extensions were floating off. She gave a sigh.

"What's the matter?" asked Bill Wong.

"It's Mrs. Raisin," said Mrs. Bloxby. "She's off again!"

Sylvan announced after half an hour that he had to leave. "I'll see you at the wedding, Agatha," he said.

"Perhaps I'll be in Paris before then," said Agatha hopefully. But Sylvan merely smiled and leaned forward and kissed her on the cheek. As soon as he had gone, Agatha realized her feet were killing her and her head was itching.

"You know," said Roy, appearing behind her, "a lot of your hair has fallen out."

Agatha took out a compact and peered in the mirror. "I'll sue that bastard," she raged.

"How did you get on with that attractive Frenchman?"

"All right," said Agatha, feeling like a fool. What must he have thought of her as she stood there, monopolizing him and losing hair right, left, and centre? Would she only be a joke to tell his friends about?

"Can you put me up for the night?" asked Roy.

"Yes, I'm taking a cab home. I've left my car in the

square, but I don't want to drive after all this champagne. Could we leave now?"

"I think you should circulate for a bit. You haven't spoken to any of your staff."

Agatha decided she had better do her social duty. She talked to Mrs. Freedman, Patrick and Phil. She moved on to Toni and Harry and asked them how they were getting on with the new agency and listened with only half an ear.

At last she decided enough was enough, collected Roy and said goodnight to James and Felicity.

At the cloakroom she collected her cloak and her bag with the flat shoes in it and slipped them on, groaning with relief.

Charles joined them. "I'm coming with you."

"If you're coming home for the night, it's the sofa for you," said Agatha.

Back in her cottage, Agatha said she was too tired to sit up discussing the party and took herself off upstairs.

As she changed out of her clothes into a nightdress and wiped off her make-up, she worried and worried that she had bored Sylvan. Had she talked too much? He had asked her about her work and she remembered she had gone on about it for a long time. But at least she would see him again. The tentacles of obsession were coiling once more around Agatha's brain.

At one point in the night, she woke up with an odd feeling of dread. She thought of Felicity and James and was overcome by a wave of fear. Something was wrong. Something was badly wrong. Then she shrugged the feeling away.

It was those shrimp canapés and champagne, thought Agatha, and then fell asleep again, dreaming of Sylvan.